Copyright © 2016 by Jamie Dossie

ISBN: 978-1-945035-05-0
Edited by Black Lyfe Publications
Cover Design by Kranchmedia
Printed in the United States of America

STOLEN MOMENTS

By Author Jamie

This story, my story, Devin Brown's story will speak to you on levels you didn't think it could. As I sit here and reminisce on the last year of my life, I can't believe it didn't happen the way we thought it would. I just knew for sure that she and I would get married have plenty of babies and live great lives at least later down the road. Life took over and none of that shit happened. Well it happened just not the way we had intended for it to.

I have a great job, I run my own landscaping company. I make great money, it's nothing I wouldn't have done for her but I fucked that shit up myself. Using Sunni to piss off Lou was never a good idea, but it seem as if I couldn't reach Lou ass no other way.

Sunni does everything her way. She don't care what the fuck it is. As long as she can do it, she will do it. No matter how much she says she loves me I know damn well she's not in love with me because I'm not in love with her, but this sham of a relationship has got to stop. Sunni is one of those, I'm rich bitch so don't say shit to me.

Lou on the other hand was my child hood crush. I have always wanted her to be my woman, but no matter what I did or what I said it didn't move her to officially be mines. It didn't stop us from finding little moments over the years to let each other know that one-day

we will be together. It didn't matter who she

was dating or who I was dating we still knew

that it would be us. Lou always had this

mentality that no one would rush her to do

anything and that's one of the reasons why we

never actually got together. I wasn't trying to

rush her but I didn't hide my love for her either.

Since Lou wasn't trying to give me no play I

settled for Sunni and boy that was a mistake,

and a lesson. No matter what a hoe trying to be,

a house wife will never work.

She believes nothing is off limits when it

comes to sex. Don't get me wrong, I love sex just

like the next man but since the very beginning,

it was always hard for me to have sex with her knowing that she was out having sex with other people, yeah I can admit it. And I let a hoe move in with me just to prove a fucking point. I truly believe in the saying, "*Be a lady in the streets and a freak in the sheets,*" but her ass is being a freak and a hoe in the streets.

I never intended to hurt Lou. I just wanted her to see that I wanted her. I've had many women and was never satisfied because they were not her. Now don't get me wrong, I never had a problem getting sex and don't foresee that shit happening. Anyway I didn't want a relationship from not one of them. They served their purpose; that's it, that's all. Until I fucked around and made Sunni feel special and Lou ran for the fucking hills. I tell you a year without her even as a friend has my life feeling different. Not one day goes pass that I haven't thought about her in some shape, form or fashion.

Sunni is always saying how much she loves me and is still very much in love with me, but we both know the real deal. The only reason she trying to hang in there is because she knows damn well if someone else finds out how much head she has given over the years randomly, (and not to say but I have heard that she's well skilled in the art of cunnilingus,) please no man will wife her but they will fuck her. Hell, it's not like I'm going to go around and tell everyone how she get down. That's her business, I just want out of it.

   I look around my house and no it's not enormous, or decked out in the finest furniture. Ours or I should say my home is very modest. It's a four bedroom family home, bedrooms are on the second level with a full bathroom. On the first level holds the living room, dining room, kitchen, family room and another full size bathroom. This home works and has been working for me for a long time. Sunni was cool with the house, she says she didn't want us to live outside our means. I guess she would say that since she spends her four million dollar inheritance on whatever the hell she wants, and let me keep the house however I want as long as it is my money that is getting spent.

Her money problems were over the day her dad died with her always being daddies little girl and her mother never being in her life. According to Sunni, her mom was always chasing the next millionaire.

Lucky for her; her rich ass daddy made his fortune in Real Estate and he had no outside kids, so it all went to her. I personally think with all the money she spends she's covering up something of her own. Hell, maybe she's just tired of my ass just as much as I'm tired of her. She will do anything to stay away from me unless she trying to find out if I'm sleeping with anyone.

The day I get the courage to live happily ever after, I'm going to make that one phone call that will change my life forever, not a minute sooner. I know what she will want of me and just having her is enough for me. I just hope she has gotten over me letting Sunni live in the very house I had always told her would be for her, and agree to have a simple conversation with me.

Louise Fields, is the only woman on this earth that has had me standing on a two-way street looking in one direction.

One

"Look Terry man just throw the damn ball. Hell we been out her for hours and you still show boating for these damn females out here on this court." You couldn't tell me nothing, I knew I was the shit on the court. Yeah, every time me and my boys hit the court it becomes pure pandemonium with the ladies. Everyone's rooting for their favorite team or in most cases their favorite man. "Man Devin don't start that shit, you know what I'm on. All these women out here, I'm bound to go home with one. Just chill and let me put on a show for the ladies."

I only had my eyes on one though and we always played the, *I see you but I don't see you routine*, it was kind of cute but two years of this shit was detrimental to a man's sex life.

My boys and I were playing a team from another Chicago neighborhood but they didn't have shit on us mainly because we had a secret weapon. Charles was the only guy who could hit three pointers with his eyes closed, with him on our team we never lost a damn game. We played at a nearby park every weekend and every weekend was the same damn thing. Terry show boated, Charles hit them threes, I just played one helluva game and everyone else did their part, that's why we the champs. Well the champs in the hood. But hey at twenty, all that matters is having money in your pocket and having a pretty girl on your arm.

I personally had many women jocking for me. Even some of them same exact women who were just trying to get at my homeboys not too long ago, I ignored shit like that. I could have been a straight up dog but getting with someone my boys was interested in was just never my thing.

I preferred the ladies who actually did have a preference in who she wanted when it came to dating or sexing. That's why my nose been wide the hell open when it comes to Louise Fields. My boys think I'm a damn fool for engaging in conversation and still not having hit it yet. All I care about is seeing her or talking to her, just being around her was always enough for me.

Oh shit! My boy Charles about to hit yet another three and we about to win this damn game! All eyes were in the air as the ball seemed to move in slow motion towards the net and all that could be heard was, "SWOOSH." We started jumping up and down as the other team congratulated us. The girls ran from the gates and from the bleachers, and hugged and kissed everyone on the team. I must say I felt some pretty damn soft lips and a hand graze pass the front of my gym shorts.

We were so excited, it was the beginning of the summer. Seems like everyone was out, school was over except for those who decided to go to junior college. I on the other hand didn't want all that college shit, my parents was pissed as hell when I told them I was going to start my own business. All they could talk about was what kind of business was I gonna start.

I looked both of them in the eye. With my money I saved my whole four years of high school, I started a landscaping service. Once I told my parents that's what I was starting they both laughed and asked where was I going to get the money? Once I told them I had the money saved from working at Foot Locker all these years. My dad put his hand on my shoulder and said, "I'll be watching." I knew what that meant, he just knew somehow I was going fuck it up, but little did he know. I had more drive than he ever had, more dreams than he ever had and shit who knows, he may be working for me one-day.

After the crowd started to disperse I saw a familiar face that I haven't seen in a month. I walked over and I hear my boys calling my name but I blocked out all the noise and kept my focus straight ahead. She was standing near the back of the court with one hand on the fence and the other one scrolling through her phone. She had on some shorts overalls, hugging her in all the right places. This girl was built like she ate collard greens and corn bread every night for dinner. Her hair was pulled into a tight pony tail with the tail of her jet black hair resting just at the top of her shoulders. Her skin look like the sun was beaming right through her. I flashed my smile, adjusted myself in my shorts and tried to keep my cool. Just with a glance she gave me and a smile I saw her cute little dimple in her right cheek.

"Hey Louise, girl you know you have a country ass name. Why the hell your parents named you that backwoods ass name?" I was smiling through every word. Just to show my humor.

"Screw you Devin! My name is from my grandmother. The strongest woman I have ever known next to my mom. So think about that the next time you try and clown my damn name." She punched me in my arm with her last statement and of course she was smiling as if she hurt me. I believe she just wanted to touch me.

"What's going on big head? I saw you out there doing your thang; I will admit you got some hops." Like I really needed her to tell me I got hops. Hell I know that, but it was still good to hear it coming from her. And did she just call me big head?

"You know that saying, "hey big head" is code for I think you cute or I like you. So which one is she saying? I have known Lou for a long while now and I know for a fact that she thinks I'm cute. I moved closer to her and eased my hand around her waist. Just to hear her little giggle. No need for you to giggle you know you like it."

Smelling her perfume she smelled like vanilla; damn she smelled sweet. I glanced over on the court and saw many of the players from both teams where hugged up with some pretty girl. If any of us are lucky we may have a story to tell tomorrow. Listening to everything she was saying was just putting me in a good mood until her fake ass boyfriend showed up.

He strolled his ass on the court and sat on the top bleacher trying to act like he wasn't watching her, but dammit I knew he was. I immediately put some space between us. She looked up towards his direction. "Looks like I have to go but I will catch up with you tomorrow." I was ready to go beat ol' boy down just for him showing up and interrupting my moment with Louise. I have many girls that approach me and I always keep them at arm's reach, looks like I need to start bringing some of them girls closer.

I watched her walk towards the bleachers until she reached him and planted the kiss that was almost mines on his lips. I shook my damn head and took my ass over where the crowd was and grab a chocolate slim beauty to cake it with. I no longer looked up in Louise direction, she could have fell backwards off the bleachers and I wouldn't have noticed. I made sure all of my attention was put into this chick who was clearly feeling me, and when she asked could I go to her house, and she slightly rubbed her perfectly round ass up against my dick; I knew what time it was. I grabbed her by the hand and we walked over to her red Camry. I tossed my athletic bag in the back seat, jumped in the front seat and headed to the South Side of Chicago. She stayed in Englewood which most would say was Death Valley. But hey, this was our hometown. Hell you look on the news and people getting shot and killed on the damn expressway. So it really didn't matter where she stayed, I was cool being there with her plus I got a few homeboys in the hood just in case some bullshit jumped off. I made a quick call to alert them that I was in the neighborhood.

When we got to her house we couldn't have been in there no longer than twenty minutes when she came from the back with a matching baby blue panty and bra set on; damn baby was stacked right. Her body was curvy in all the right places, not too big or too small, and I was about to touch all over her ass…literally.

Once we got back to her room I had her speaking in tongues. I let my mouth explore every inch of her body. Just from the way she was shaking and trembling, I knew right there and then, she had never had a snake tongue like mines. I had her legs up over her damn head pounding into her so damn deep, yup and that's when I saw it. That one tear that trickles out of a woman's eye when you are hitting her spot over and over again.

Two

I was pissed the hell off, I can't even front. Yeah so what that David brought his ass to the court unannounced. But dammit when I saw Devin ass all hugged up with that chocolate sistah I was ready to scream. Like who the fuck is she? Where the fuck did she come from? Nine times out of ten he probably was hugged up on her just to piss me off…and it worked. I'm sick and tired of this two year merry-go-round. For whatever reasons it seem as if we can't get our shit together, but like we been doing, I'm gonna keep doing me and from the looks of it Devin ass is gonna keep doing him.

If I didn't have to work today at my mom's bakery I would go to his house and ask him a few questions. I simply don't like the fact that he tried to play me just because he was feeling some type of way. But if this is what things are going to come to, then I may keep David around a little longer, just in case I need him to show up at a party or something, just to show Devin ass that I'm not alone. I don't know anybody who is going to play these games with him; surely not me.

Seeing him a couple days ago did feel good though. I haven't seen him in a month only because I went to Miami to visit a childhood friend of mine. She moved there for school a year ago and now she swears she will never come back to Chicago and actually I can't blame her. Hell I know damn well, I want to get out of here my damn self. I just really don't know where I want to go, I was born and raised here and I don't want to continue to live here forever. I'm glad she had the guts to push forward with her dreams. But honestly, I like working in the family business, it's only me and my mom. She opened her bakery about seven years ago, I was thirteen at the time. I don't think I have ever seen my mom this happy until the day she cut the ribbon on her shop. I wasn't big enough to ring up the customers, momma thought I would mess up the count or something, but it soon was after she saw I had an A in math that I was thrown onto the register. Outside of that I was right by her side helping out, that's what I do to this day when I'm not doing all the other things she got me doing up in here. She's always saying, "Louise this is gonna be your shop one-day." All I could do is smile and give her a hug because I knew no matter what, she wanted the best for me.

Maybe one-day Devin and I will get it together. It seems like we do a lot of talking and hugging and even some little kisses along the way, but not much else. He always seems to have some chick he is liking on or I'm dealing with some guy but we never seem to deal with each other.

I mean he stands at six feet even, dark smooth skin, pretty ass teeth and because he always played sports his body frame was strong and lean.

All I could do is smile at the mere mention of his name, we practically grew up together. We met when we were eight, went to the same school Grammar and High School, we were like the best of friends. I have never had a guy to be a best friend. Always a friend who wanted some ass but never a best friend who never pushed up on me every chance he got. Don't get me wrong he has tried. Hell, we both have, and till this day I hold that special in my heart. But don't get me wrong, if we ever get to the point of sexing, oh yeah he getting it.

Fuck it! I have waited and this shit is really bothering me. I said I wasn't going to call but fuck it. I grab my S6 off the dining room table, walked to the front porch and sat in one of the wooden chairs. Crossed my legs, searched through my call log and press his number. It rang three times before he picked up.

"Oh wow! I just knew I would've heard from you way before now!" Oh see that's why I didn't want to call because I knew he would be expecting it.

"Well I figured I would give you a couple days to wash off the stench of that chick you just all of a sudden got so damn interested in. "

"Oh so in other words you were mad?"

No he didn't! "I wasn't mad."

"Girl please! You don't get to know someone for twelve years and don't know when they are pissed, and it's not like it's the first time you started tripping when you have seen me with someone else."

"Devin, please what about all the times you get mad when you see me with someone else; who ain't, you!"

"Louise, please! Don't try and turn this shit around. The only reason you even on my line is because you want to indirectly ask for info of what may have happened between me and Chell."

"Oh that's her name?"

"Yes."

"I can pretty much guess what happened. All you guys are cock hounds anyway."

"Just like David, huh?"

"We not talking about him."

"Shit! Now we are."

"How the hell did he get into a conversation about us when were primarily talking about you?"

"See Lou, that's your problem right there. As long as we talking about me and my shit you cool, but as soon as the attention is put back on you; you get shook."

This dude knows damn well he gets on my fucking nerves. He think he's right about every damn thing and most of the damn time he's wrong. Fuck I could just scream right now!

"Fuck it Devin! I'm ending this conversation."

"I figured you would. Hey the truth hurts doesn't it? Well since you ending this one, let's start another one. When you leave the bakery tonight what you got planned?"

Look at him he does this shit every time he knows he has pissed me off, then turn around and ask me what I am doing.

"Well since its Sunday I'll be at the bakery by myself. So once I close up and everything I'm just gonna hang out at home. Momma gone on her weekend gambling trip; she'll be back tomorrow.

"Can I come chill later?"

"Your big headed ass gets on my damn nerves, but yeah." Damn I swear I heard his smile through the phone. I can also kick myself for being so damn weak.

"I knew you would say that; see you later."

Right after that the phone just went dead. I held the phone in my hand for a moment and simply laughed at our behavior. He has always had a way of getting up under my skin then acting like nothing happened and expect me to kick it with him as usual. One of these damn days I'm gonna surprise his ass and he is going to have to find something else to occupy his time.

Three

I was excited to see Devin later on. No matter how much we try and fight it, there is and always have been something irresistible between us. It's only been the last two years that we been playing duck-duck- goose. We are truly pieces of each other. We complement each other there is no doubt about that. Hell even our friends see it and as always we say, "we just friends" which is true. I just don't know how much is the "just" part is true.

After locking up the bakery I was back at home no later than nine; it was breezy and warm outside. Everywhere I turned cars were rolling down the street bumping everything from old school, house music, slow jams, you name it; it was being played. You could pretty much tell the kind of mood people were in by the kind of music they were playing.

I walked up on my porch and the very dude that makes sure he speak to me all day every day yelled out, "Hey Ms. Lady. You looking good today, as usual." I thanked him for the compliment and walked my ass in the house. I looked around the house, of course it was clean. I ordered some hot wings and pizza, as always the food will be here before he will. I know I had just about an hour before he showed up.

I showered and changed into a pair of dark blue jean shorts. A keep Calm and Love tee-shirt, a pair of red flip-flops, threw a head band on my head, took a look at myself in the full length mirror and wondered why in the hell do I even care what I look like to a...friend? I was done and fifteen minutes after that the food arrived, thirty minutes after that Devin come strolling up, I was already sitting on the porch when he got out of his boys Kevin car, "Hey Lou!" I spoke back to Kevin before he peeled away from the curb.

"Took you long enough, did you bring the Pepsi?"

"Girl quit playing. What the hell you think in this damn bag? It sure ain't my laundry."

"I'm just making sure. You do have a tendency to forget shit, especially if you up in some big booty, small waist chick face." Damn all of two minutes she has found a way to bring up another woman. Glad I'm prepared for this.

"Well since I didn't forget, I guess I wasn't in anyone's face. Cause if so, you'd be drinking on water with them hot wings."

"Whatever! Do you want to sit out here or go in the house?"

"We can chill out here. It feels too good out here to go in the house."

I was going to hook up my phone to the speaker and play some music but courtesy of my neighbors across the street blasting their music; we were set. The summer air was nice; the breeze even better. We both were bobbing our heads to the music eating hot wings and pizza. This is really turning out to be a great Sunday evening. I glanced over at him about a hundred times. I noticed he didn't even look at his phone once, he was engaged in conversation with me about any and everything. Nothing mattered at this point, as long as we were together that was all that mattered in my book.

"So Lou, are you serious with the dude that came by the court the other day?"

Oh shit! I knew this was coming and as much as I grilled him about the girls he be hanging around with, I knew at some point he was going to hit me with this. I could either ignore his question but then I won't be able to ask him nothing else.

"We not serious. We have hung out a few times, tripped out, you know that sort of thing."

"Have you had sex with him?" I almost choked on my damn chicken when that question came flying out of his mouth.

"Well if you must know. Yes, we have had sex twice."

Devin kept looking ahead hearing every word I spoke but he didn't look in my direction except to only ask me a question. I on the other hand kept my face glued in his direction while I fumbled with a hot wing. I felt bad as hell but he and I have a no lie policy. No matter who else we lie to, we will not lie nor disrespect each other. He took a deep breath took another slice of pizza and changed the subject just like that. From past conversations we have had, whenever he does that; it generally means that he is silently pissed off. I wanted to scream at him for knowing he was pissed, especially when he knows I know, he slept with that girl just a couple of days ago.

Silence filled the air.

I started to act like cars coming down the street was more entertaining than being there with him. I really didn't know what to say since he had messed the mood up. So I just started talking about some random stuff.

"So our birthdays are next month, you want to throw a big 21 bash like we always planned? I think it will be off the chain, we're finally going to be grown and get to do what the hell we want!" I was wailing my arms in the air and snapping my fingers and all I heard was crickets on his end. He still hadn't looked my way since he asked me that bullshit ass question so I waited a minute before I hopped out the chair and took my happy ass in the house.

I waved at a few folks across the street and left Devin ass sitting on the porch. This shit was ridiculous and I wasn't about to feed into this crap. I had to be in the house about forty-five minutes before he strolled his ass in. I was in the back which we call the family room. I heard him go to the bathroom down the hall from the family room. I had totally got my mind off of him and his bullshit. I'm laughing hard at the movie Soul Men with Bernie Mac. Damn, this movie had me laughing so hard and I've seen it over ten times. Anyone would think I had never seen it in my life. I looked to my left and Devin was standing his ass in the door way with his arms crossed in front of his chest watching me like I'm prey or something.

"May I help you?" I didn't know what he was about to say but I knew he needed to make it good or else this was going be a short night for us.

"I'm just trying to figure out why does it seems like you sleep with every man you so called get with? I mean damn! I like sex just as much as the next man but I don't think you realize that I ask you this same question every time I see you with some new dude, and you always seem to disappoint me by giving that same damn answer you just gave tonight." His tone was low but serious and I couldn't believe this dude, who I assume would fuck anything with two legs and a greasy split, coming at me like we having sex!

I smiled a half smile and got instantly pissed off, how in the hell is he going to come for me when I didn't send for him. I tell you these dudes out here be thinking they own you and shit, and I'm simply not having this shit from him and no one else! I stood up and walked towards the doorway and stood about two feet from him. Balanced my weight on my right leg and placed my left hand on my hip.

"So what you asked the same damn question and received the same damn answer! Sounds to me like you need to quit asking me questions that you really don't want to know the answer to!"

"Oh I wanted to know them. I just didn't realize you were sitting on every dick you came across!"

"You son-of-a-bitch! You got some damn nerve! You can sleep with whoever you want but when I do it; it's a problem. Ain't that a bitch!"

"Say what you want Lou, but honestly it's not a good look and the shit is not pretty in no kind of way." This dude was still leaning up against the doorway now with his hands to his sides. I was furious! I couldn't believe this shit was happening. If this was what he came over here for he could have kept his ass at home.

"Honestly? Really? The only reason you tripping is because out of all the dudes, you're pissed because you have not been one to slide inside of me. Now that's some truth for your ass! Now either deal with it or leave me the fuck alone with this bullshit!" I saw him frown, his brows were drawn together, his lips were tight and his right hand was bald into a fist.

"See that's the problem with your ass, instead of listening when I'm telling you something, you try and flip the shit on me but not this time Lou, not this time. He looked like he was about to turn and walk away; then he stopped. I'm tired of this rollercoaster Lou and if I said anything that has hurt your feelings I'm sorry but I meant every word I said. He began to walk away and I grabbed him by his arm. I just couldn't let him walk away like this, we have been friends far too long for this shit to end like this. It was fine when we were teenagers but being adults there has to be a better way. No haps Lou, too much has been said and we should just end the night and regroup before the spewing of words seriously hurts someone and then it can't be undone." He had a sadden look on his face, one I've seen before and I couldn't let him leave like this.

I walked up to him and planted one of the most passionate kisses I could eject out of me. It was only when I felt his lips part that I knew he was into the kiss. This felt so right. I have kissed him many times before but this time was so romantic and passionate. It was one of those make up kisses. He palmed my ass as I wrapped my arms around his neck, he pinned me up against the wall rubbing his hands up and down my full breast. My breathing was heavy with passion, his touch was damn near orgasmic. Our shirts decorated the floor, my right leg was wrapped around his waist and just as I went and tugged at his shorts, he grabbed my hand. He looked at me with all the desire that he had towards me, kissed my lips and let my leg down gently.

"Devin, what's wrong?" My voice was melancholy. I didn't know what was happening. One moment we were on a roll and now he's picking his shirt up off the floor.

"Baby, as bad as I want to finally feel you and experience a night of passion with you, this damn sure is not how I want it to happen. All that shit that was said between us and I know you ready to give me the prize, and like any man I'm ready to take it. Not like this Lou."

"Devin wait are you serious?" He was a few more steps from the door and I just knew this shit wasn't happening after all this time. I just knew it was finally about to happen.

"I'm damn dead serious. Look how we just went off on each other. That shit isn't going to do nothing but intensify after we have sex and personally I don't want no parts of that shit. I will call you tomorrow."

This dude has left me standing in the middle of my damn floor panting like a horny ass dog. Did this nigga just walk out the door like for real? This type of shit just don't happen to me but I see he want to be different and shit. I grabbed my shirt off the floor, went out on the porch and by the time I was able to get to the side walk and looked both ways; he was gone.

Four

That was one of the hardest things I ever had to do. To walk away from the only woman I have ever loved and the only woman I truly wish was mine but the very thought of her and other dudes so frequent blows my fucking mind. I can't even front that shit hurts. When I come across some dude that she has been with, like most niggas who want to boast, he starts hinting around on what kind of woman she is in the bedroom and I simply can't listen to that shit. I see how she is when she is able to just hop from one person to the next, whenever the wind blows and I'll be damn if I just gonna become another notch on her belt.

This woman gets bored with just about anything that comes across her path. She's ready for the next best thing and I don't want to be with her one-day and she gets bored with my ass, oh hell no! Waking up this morning, I felt like I'm damned if I do sleep with her and I am damned if I don't. I know she's pissed off, hell I'm pissed off but I'll be damn if we become fuck buddies. Hell we already got that shit with other people. Some folks just don't fit that realm of people, at least not for me.

I glanced over at my clock on the night stand and it read 7 a.m. I couldn't believe I was up. My first landscaping appointment wasn't until one o'clock, but laying here with Stephanie; I was ready for her to wake up and get out. I walked into her as I walked home from Lou house, she was on her way to a party. She invited me to go and I wasn't interested at the time but after ending things with Lou the way we did, I had some built up frustration I had to get out and best believe I took it out on her sweet little ass. Now that's all out of my system, she needs to roll. I mean friends with benefits are supposed to cum and then go. Plus I had Lou on the brain so damn hard this morning I couldn't even lay there and sleep. Once you get a good nut you are supposed to fall asleep…not in this case.

I know for a fact she was hurt. The look in her eyes would haunt me for a while and that's a look I don't want to continue to put on her face.

I figured I would do the test by texting her and if

she texted back then I would call.

Good Morning beautiful, I hope you are

okay.

I pressed the send button, the way my palms

was sweating you would think I was about to

have major surgery. I slid out the bed and

walked around my studio and went to look out

the window. The streets where clear, not a peep

from no one. The block was calm but hell it

wouldn't be for long; folks still in the bed. I

grabbed the remote and cut on the news. I had

the volume down low. I really just wanted to see

the weather and just as I cut it on, the weather

showed that it would be 82 degrees today. I heard Stephanie fumbling behind me as she walked to the bathroom. I kept my attention on the news not hearing a thing they were saying. I heard the shower run. I already had clean towels and I always kept Caress or Dove under the sink, I know women don't want to smell like no man. Fifteen minutes later she emerged from the bathroom and started putting on her clothes.

"Thank you for a wonderful time last night Devin. I really needed that." I have to hand it to her she knew how to play the fuck buddy role. I turned the T.V. off turned and looked t her.

"Not a problem. I'm just glad you answered when I called. Other than that it would have been a long and hard night for me. So I really should be thanking you." She grabbed her purse and sunglasses off of the chair that sat next to the bed.

"Don't be a stranger Devin." With that she walked out the front door. I watched her through the blinds as she jumped in to her black Altima. Damn nice car! Wonder what dude got that for her?

I grabbed my phone and just looked at it, I wanted to call Lou so damn bad just to get some resolution about last night. I just knew she was going to be pissed and I really didn't want to deal with her and her attitude so damn early this morning; sometimes I got to take her ass in doses. "Fuck it!" I went to my call log scrolled down and pushed her number it was now or never. After the second ring she answered.

"Hello."

"Good morning Lou, I texted you but I got no response."

"Well you got me now. What's up?" Damn she can be so damn cold at times.

"Well with what happened last night, I just wanted to make sure you were okay."

"Why wouldn't I be? I mean you're the one who practically ran out, so fuck it. I'm cool trust me." Cool my ass I'm sitting here listening to her and I swear she's about to go off.

"I was just checking and I told you why I left. If I hadn't, we would have been rolling around on the floor slapping bellies.'

"And that's a bad thing?"

"Lou let me ask you something, with the male friends you are entertaining are you ready to give them up?"

"I guess we would never know now, especially since you decided to make my mind up for me. Hell while you asking me, are you ready to give up your stains?" I knew she wasn't going to give me a straight answer. She'll go all around it and once again find a way to put it on me.

"See that's just that; they are stains. People I get with, bust a nut and move on. I don't have a woman and I'm not in a relationship of any kind and trust any woman I deal with on a sexual level will know her place, and if she can't hang then she must move on. See the difference between us is I would love to have a relationship with you and you been running from me for the last two years and that's mainly because you my love are not ready to let go of the men that are in your life."

Fuck this! I was sick and tired of her always going around a question so she don't have to give me the answer that I just gave her, and she don't have to. I'm a man who knows women enough to know when they want you, they will come for you and when they don't they won't. I know she wants me but she wants me to sit in the corner so she can pull me out when she ready and that shit is not about to happen.

"Okay, so what if I'm not ready to be in a full time relationship! That doesn't make be a bad person dammit! Hell we are only twenty years old about to hit the big twenty-one, and you on my ass about not wanting to be in a relationship with you. You obviously got me fucked up. Yes I do enjoy the time I have with my other male friends at least they are not putting me through this bullshit. And you're supposed to be my best friend, the one I haven't slept with."

"That's some funny shit because just last night you were ready to change all of that shit!"

"Yes I was, because I was sure you would be able to handle sexing me and being my friend without all the extras." This woman is truly something else she know damn well after I dick her down and she saw me later with some other chick she would lose her fucking mind. She'll never admit to it though.

"Okay Lou, seems like you're doing well and I see this conversation is getting us nowhere. So I will holla at you in a couple of days." I hung up without even wanting to hear another word from her. She knows damn well she can get on my nerves. Maybe one-day she will understand where I'm coming from, until then, hell I'm going to continue to do me and let her do her.

Five

I did not expect to hear this shit. He was barking so damn early this morning. Hell there's better things to do other than this, and if I had of played my cards right; I would have been doing just that. As I sat on my Queen size bed, covered by only a sheet, I thought about everything that Devin was talking about, and I thought we would have gotten together by now but it has never happened. Like I told him I truly love being able to do me, I don't want to have to answer to him and no one else for that matter.

Sometimes I just wish we had of just went on ahead and had sex and moved on, then that crap wouldn't be hanging over our heads. David and I are just friends, just like so many other people in my life. I like to have options and if I got in a relationship with Devin all my options go out the window, unless I cheat and who wants to do that shit. I just hate that he thinks I'm keeping him in a corner and pulls him out only when I feel it is necessary. At some point we are going have to talk about this and move on.

I smelled bacon, French toast, and scrambled eggs. I knew momma was coming home today from her gambling trip, I just had no idea she would be here so soon. I walked down the stairs in a pair of pink striped shorts and a black tank top that I had slept in. I made my way to the kitchen and saw momma standing over the stove flipping French toast.

"Good Morning sweet pea. It's about time you came downstairs. I was beginning to think that you were going to have to warm your breakfast up."

I walked over to my mom and kissed her on her cheek and gave her a great big hug. Just having her home made me feel better and knowing her food was going to hit the right spot.

"I had no idea you were coming home so soon." I sat at the round wooden kitchen table watching momma move swiftly throughout the kitchen.

"Chile, those nags started arguing over who called bingo first and all hell broke loose, so the coordinator of the trip shorten it and I couldn't have been more happy. I won thirty-five hundred the first day we got there and I was done. I played a few quarters on the slots but broke even, so yeah I was ready to come home. How did everything go at the shop while I was gone?"

I shook my head because she ask me the same question every single time she go somewhere and like always I tell her all went well.

"As usual momma everything went well. So I know I can get a few dollars off that thirty-five…right momma?" She turned back to the stove like she didn't even hear one word I said but if I know my momma, she was just figuring out how much she was going to actually give me.

"Grab a couple plates out of that cabinet so we can eat this breakfast I've prepared for us. Oh your birthday is a month away, are you and Devin going to still have that big birthday bash y'all have always talked about?"

I couldn't do nothing but sigh and look down. I was feeling some kind of way behind this and I must admit that his words did hit me below the belt. Being the tuff ass I show on the outside, his words was like a piping hot sword that sliced through me like butter.

"Well momma to be honest we had another argument and now we aren't speaking, it may be a few days or longer before we do. So I don't know what may happen come July 14th. I hope we still have a party like we have been planning ever since we were sixteen, but who knows."

I looked at my momma, she threw her kitchen towel over her shoulder as she grabbed a plate from the table. She said a, "hmmm" here and there, whenever she does that she normally is thinking really hard. I don't really want to hear any of her so called constructive criticism. She had everything she had cooked on my plate.

Then she reached for the other plate and piled it

high, sat down right across from me, said a

silent prayer and then she looked at me. I knew

it was coming.

"First let me say you and Devin have been

knowing each other for a long time and you two

have been arguing just as long. Now what you

have to ask yourself is. Are the arguments and

him worth it? You don't even have to tell me

what the argument was about this time but all I

know is that boy has been sniffing around here

and most of the time you ignore him." I wanted

to cut her off right then and there because I

don't think I ignore him at all. But if I open that

door, momma is going to go somewhere I don't even want to go so I will just listen to her.

"I hear what you saying momma, I really do but I'm just getting tired of these arguments, I mean we are friends we shouldn't be arguing like we do."

"Says who?"

"Momma you know what I mean."

"No I don't. Make it plain."

"As friends we shouldn't be arguing like we are in a relationship."

All my momma did was start snickering. She placed a piece of bacon in her mouth and looked at me and smiled. She took a few more bites of food took a sip of her piping hot coffee before she said another word.

"Darling, I hate to be the bearer of bad news but you two have been in a relationship for a while now and even through you both want to use the term, friends, it still doesn't stop the fact that you two are in fact in a relationship. Now if that's what you don't want, you better tell him but don't get pissed when he ends up with someone else. Just a little advice from momma. Now go on ahead and eat your food, it's getting cold."

I couldn't say nothing else even if I wanted to, momma kind of went over my head on this one. That's all we are is friends, I must be missing something but to let momma tell it she knows what she is talking about. We finished talking and I was told that I would be working the bakery by myself today which isn't a problem. I knew she was going to say it so I just prepared myself for it.

Around twelve I hopped in mommas grey Kia Sophia and headed to the bakery. She called it "Lou-Lou's Sweets," after me. I waved at a few friends and associates as I headed down Chicago Ave. I opened up the shop and within an hour the shop was crowed. No matter what, folks in the neighborhood loved my momma's baked goods. We decided to have the bakery designed where people could order something, sit in a little nook or booth or a round table, read the paper or grab some books from our library that we started with great up and coming Authors in the Midwest area. We also had many books from other authors from other cities and states as well. Lou-Lou's was just a great hang out spot.

As I was talking to one of the other customers the phone rang. I excused myself and took an order of twelve red velvet cupcakes, twelve double chocolate cupcakes, and they stated that it was for a pick-up in an hour. I assured the customer that the order would be ready within the hour. I hung up and got right to making her order. Between getting the order ready and getting back to the register to ring up customers as they came through the door, it was a wonder how I finished in time; but I did.

There was laughter and chatter throughout the bakery. It felt good to look at a business that you have and people actually enjoy it. I was just about to walk to the back to refill the shelves, when a young lady walked in looking somewhat confused.

"Hi, welcome to Lou-Lou's Sweets, how may I help you?" I extended my hand and greeted her with a fabulous smile.

"Hi, I called about an hour ago and placed the red velvet and double chocolate cupcakes twelve of each."

"Oh! Okay I have your order in the back, I'll be right back."

I walked to the back and grabbed two medium sized boxes with a see through window so the customer can take a peek at their order. And I through in a small box of twelve mini's of different flavors we also carry. It's something we do for all of our new customers.

"All right here's your order. How would you like to pay for it?"

"Um, do you take credit cards?"

"Yes we do." She handed me her card and I handed her back a receipt for her to sign. After the transaction was over I went on to explain the free mini cupcakes that I hoped she would enjoy.

She let me know that she was new to Chicago. She lived in Texas all of her life. After her dad passed away a few months back she decided to settle on living in one of the houses he had here in Chicago. I made an announcement in the bakery asking everyone to give her a warm Chi-town welcome. As light as she was she turned as red as a tomato, I didn't mean to embarrass her. I just wanted her to feel the love.

"Thanks for such a warm welcome, my name is Sunni."

She looked like the sun too, she was at least 5'4", light bright, she had short wavy hair, she had more breast than booty but overall she would be considered attractive to many men. Especially from the ones I see sitting in this very shop.

"Let me get these home, I'm having a small get together at my home and guest will be arriving soon. I saw your flyer in the grocery store on a bulletin board and since I don't know who the go to around here is, I came here."

"I appreciate your business. Enjoy your samples and don't be a stranger as you can see this is a great hangout spot."

"I'll remember that and thanks again."

With that she was gone but not for long.

Six

Five days had gone pass and I dared not to even pick up the phone to call Lou. I just didn't want to even go through the back and forth with her. My birthday is in a few weeks, so my main focus is women and drinking. Fuck it; I will no longer worry about a woman who is so into other dudes that she can't even see straight.

Now that I think about it, I should have banged the hell out of her and watched her lose her mind when I'm with another woman. Oh yeah she would have acted like nothing happened but then she would have been blowing my phone up and texting me like she just been kidnapped. I'm not going for none but somehow she would've found a way to put this all on me.

I grabbed my gym bag and my basketball and walked out the house into the hot awaiting sun. Chicago summers don't be playing. I covered my eyes with my left hand and used it as a visor briefly, as I fished through my bag to grab my sunglasses. I began my four block walk to the court when I saw this very attractive woman walking with a bunch of other women. Her complexion was deep chocolate, she had her hair in small twist, even though she was on the heavy side for my liking; this woman was simply breathtaking. I was about to cross the street when I didn't even have the light and a black mustang blew its horn in my direction. It scared the hell out of me but snapped me out of my trance. I walked a few more blocks and to my surprise they seem to be going the same way I was going.

All I could think was please be heading to the court. I needed a distraction from Lou, and she seemed to be just what I needed. If you looked at a group of women most would say she was the overweight dark skinned one out the group, in other words they would have thought she was ugly, but not in my eyes her beauty jumped at me and what I normally wasn't use to immediately became intriguing.

I looked ahead about a block and a half and saw the court was full, I started walking a little faster. I didn't want to be late, everyone who knows me knows, this was when I shined the most. The court was my hoe and I was the pimp. She gave me everything I needed, every single time. I looked up and did a light jog across the street, approaching the court I slung my bag to the right near the bleachers and who the fuck do I see on the very top bleacher, Lou ass. I did a slight wave so we wouldn't have to go through the why you didn't speak song and dance. On the other side of the court the group of women I saw looking like they're ranging from the ages of nineteen through twenty –two sat on the bleachers cheering and laughing extremely loud. I peeped shorty looking at me and I gave her ass the eye to let her know she was on my radar.

I adjusted my gym shorts, put my band around my head, slapped five with my homies and got ready to play some fucking ball. Cars were parked along the curbs of the court and people were hanging outside their cars, some sitting on the hood of the car waiting to see a great game, as only my homies and I could give. The other team came all the way from the hundreds to whoop our asses. Too bad they had no idea we don't take ass whooping's; we only give them out.

Game on! We ran circles around the guest. Every basket made me and my homies were either slapping five, fist pumping, or what we really like to do is talk mo' shit than a little bit. All the young women in the neighborhood were like our own personal cheerleaders. I heard my boy Keith say, "That's some bullshit!" The ref didn't catch this dude. They call Rob for traveling from the guest team.

"Oh hell no! That motherfucker just traveled and the ref didn't catch that shit; talking about he didn't see it! Fuck that! I saw it and so did other people. Man this is some bullshit! Who hired this bum ass ref anyway?" Keith was on one, he was just as serious as I am when it comes to this ball thing. Everyone trying to calm him down and the ref trying to go hard like fuck us, and what my boy thought he saw.

"You little punk ass nigga! I will whoop your ass on this court! I see shit the way I see it and I didn't see that, you need to get your eyes checked lil nigga! People from the sideline was holding the ref back, we were holding Keith back. We only had five more minutes in the game and we were up by ten. I didn't give a fuck we could have thrown in the towel; it's not like they were going to win anyway.

I shouted out, "Do y'all want to keep going to the end or you want to just be done with it?" To my surprise they wanted to finish, we didn't have another ref so we used who we had. Everyone took a two minute time-out, once everyone got their shit right, we hit the court hard and in five minutes the guest team was down by sixteen. Got to hand it to them, they tried but we will not get beat on our home court.

Keith and some of the other homies were still going off about the ref fucking up a call. I was done with that and on to something else. Music was blaring from the cars that was parked along the side. It was a twerk contest on the court, lord all the ass I saw. Shit I was ready to bust right then and there. But I saw the same group of girls. At least four of them seem to be in on the twerk contest but the chocolate honey I had my eye on was standing on the sideline just watching her crazy, hot in the ass friends. I glanced back over to the other side of the bleachers and saw Lou talking to one of the dudes from the losing team. I laughed inside thinking she could have at least chopped it up with a nigga on a winning team, I smiled and walked on over to put my mouth piece to work.

When she saw me approaching she smiled so damn big. I could already tell she was feeling me and she knew I was feeling her. We walked to the bleachers sat down and chopped it up. I found out that she's the cousin of one the girls in the groups and she would only be here for a few weeks. She is originally from Minnesota. I laughed at the thought of how I was going take her down whether she knew it or not.

I walked off with my chocolate honey who name is Naomi. She said her mom always thought she looked like the model so found it was only right that she named her after one. She wore a cute little Nike's short outfit with a pair of all white Nikes. She wasn't flashy or anything, she just was cool and I was going to make the best of these few weeks.

We walked off, I walked to the other side and left her standing by the gate to get my gym bag. Lou was still standing there talking to that busta and I know damn well she was looking at me.

Sure enough, I will hear about this. Maybe not tonight, not even tomorrow; but I will hear about it. Either way I was cool with it. Naomi and I went to get something to eat and just find out as much as we could about each other in such a short time. I wanted to take her to my place and really get to know her but I thought I would wait a day or two; see if she's really down to get dicked down.

Just as planned a couple of days went passed and shorty was tangled in my covers acting like I was the best she ever had. Now don't get me wrong, I do a damn good job when it comes to slapping bellies, but she was either acting…poorly or she really hadn't had no great dick. She put more hickeys on my neck and chest than any woman ever has. Even when I was in my early teens bumping and grinding I didn't have these many hickeys, but I was cool with it. She knew she wasn't my woman but like most women she wanted others to know that she was in my bed. Hell I was cool with it, I don't have anyone to answer to and I wish like hell anyone tried to get crazy.

A week had passed and me and lil momma been hanging. She didn't have much to do so I even brought her along a couple of times with me to a couple of jobs. She was cool with it all and she cut my work time in half. With that we did the usual stuff movies, dinner, drink, just enjoying each other with no attachments. Lou called me a time a two and that was only because she probably has heard about me and Naomi. I mean, she be with me when I'm on the court and anyone who is anyone was always there. If you had any business that you didn't want anyone to know about as a rule on the street…don't do it on the court.

It's been a week since I had said anything to Lou and I was figuring it was time that we talked. I really didn't want to talk, I just wanted to let her know that I was around. So I sent a text.

Hey Lou, I was thinking if we doing a bash for our birthdays then we need to start

planning something. It's only weeks away. Get at me when you can.

I know in my heart she looking at that text ready to spit fire. Hell I know how to get in where I fit in, and I was not hanging around Lou ass like that anymore. If she want to fuck with me, she's going to have to come to me. Until then, shit I'm going to keep wearing my catcher's mit and catch all the greasy splits that's been coming my way.

Twenty minutes passed and still no text from Lou. I threw my phone down on the bed and went to take a shower. I been working and balling all week and I was going to just chill at the crib for the rest of the night even though the streets was live as hot wire. I gave it a second thought knowing it was always women on every block looking to be seen. Hell, I'm even tired of that right now. I just need to chill tonight and get back on it tomorrow. I cut the shower on full blast just as I was about to step in my phone did a quick double beep. I just knew it was Lou.

I ran my ass to the bed eager to hear from her, grabbed the phone and read the text.

I'm only here for a few more days. If you're not busy can I come over and keep you company? This is Naomi.

I smiled and replied back.

Be on your way!

I quickly texted her my address ran back to the shower, this was going to be a great night after all!

Happy Birthday to Us

I woke up to birds chirping outside my window, the sun shining through as if it was my very own special alarm clock waking me up on this very special day. Wow, I can't believe I'm finally twenty-one today, I know damn well Devin ass is up and probably with a some chick in his bed, but that shit is none of my business.

We have only talked a few times and it was mainly to make plans about our birthday party. I must admit even though we aren't really talking it was strange making plans with him, not really knowing if he wanted to do this or if he felt obligated to do so.

I've seen him on the court with some extra thick sistah acting like he didn't even see me sitting on the bleachers, but it's whatever because I damn sure wasn't alone. I jumped out of bed straighten out my shorts and tank top, grabbed my phone off of the dresser, went through my call log and pressed Devin's name. On the second ring he answered.

"Happy fucking Birthday Lou! Man we finally made it. Our all white party is going to be the bomb tonight! I'm so fucking excited! We have planned this shit for years. What you doing right now?"

Damn I couldn't even get a word in. I didn't know whether or not he was excited to talk to me or because it was our birthday. It's like he didn't take a breath during his whole conversation. This was a totally different Devin than I have been used to for the last past week or so.

"Happy Birthday Devin! Hell yeah we finally made it! I'm just glad we made up so we can have our birthday bash together. And actually I just got out of the bed. What's up?"

"I'm going to come get you and take you to Grand Lux for breakfast, so get ready, I will be there in about forty minutes. Get ready now!"

With that, the phone clicked off. I smiled from ear to ear. I was glad to have my friend back, I needed to have him back in life. Most people when they don't have anything to do, they get bored or simply find something much less pleasing. But *with* me and Devin, we always have a good time together and when we don't want to be bothered by the outside world, we simply come together and enjoy each other's company. It's no one on this earth that I can say I would love to spend time like that.

I got ready in the nick of time. I threw on some form fitting black capris, a black V neck fitted tee-shirt and a pair of wedges. Nothing special, but cute. I ran down stairs just to have momma meet me on the front porch as I approached.

"There's my grown baby. Just look at you, seems just like yesterday I was putting pigtails in your hair and wiping the ice cream from your mouth. And now look at you, all grown up."

My momma was about to make me cry she always said the mushiest stuff anyone has ever heard. Just to be in her embrace at this very moment was the best birthday gift I could ever have.

"Thank you so much momma. You're about to have me crying on my birthday and it's just ten in the morning." We shared a laughed then momma reached behind her and grabbed a folded up piece of paper that sat on the wooden round table that sat on the porch. I looked wondering what it could have been and what could have her in tears.

"Lou, I have waited for this day for a while now and I am not getting any younger so I pass the torch to you." I had a look of confusion, I drew my brows together and didn't know what to make of this. So I just opened the paper and read it word for word.

My mouth fell open; I covered it with my left hand and continued to read. My momma has managed to make me cry when I have been trying hard not to.

"Momma I can't believe you, are you serious? I mean this can't be. I'm truly at a loss for words."

"Well baby it is your birthday and I told you this day was coming. I have done my part to get you here, it's all up to you now." All I could do at that moment was hug my mom and wipe the tears from my eyes.

I looked back at the papers and a loud car horn brought me out of my trance. I looked back and forth from the paper and the street to see who was making all this noise so early in the morning.

Devin ass started laying on the horn like the bulls just won the championship. You could see his bright smile from the car. It felt so damn good to see him and I couldn't wait to tell him the good news. Devin parked and hopped out the car, and walked over to the porch where mom and I were sitting.

"Hey mom. What up Lou? Girl it's our day we are about to get it in!" Devin hugged and kissed both mom and I. This man was so damn excited that it was unreal. This was an awesome feeling.

"You looking good son, how is business going for you? And how are your parents? I haven't seen them in a while."

"My family good momma. You know my dad still wishes I would just go to college and drop my business, but mom is cool with it all. She likes the idea that I started my own business; but other than that, I have been real good."

"That's real good son. You keep doing what you doing. If it makes you happy, stay with it. Not many people your age can say they have their own business; so if you ask me you are on the right path."

Momma treated him just like her own. She smiled so hard with every word she spoke. Momma was genuinely proud of him which excited me so damn much, I instantly started seeing him in another light.

"Thank you so much momma. Hearing those words was something I really needed to hear. I truly love you for your kind words."

"Alright now all this mushy stuff has got to stop y'all! I got good news to share while we are all in such a good mood. Momma has signed the bakery over to me, look at this! This is a dream come true for me."

Devin snatched the paper out of my hand and read the words just as I did minutes ago. His eyes lit up like a damn Christmas tree, he started smiling hard, which lead momma and I to do the same. Devin hugged us both and then congratulated me. This was going to be an amazing day, I was ready to get things under way.

"Alright momma, I'm about to take your daughter out for her birthday breakfast. I hope to see you before we go out and party tonight."

"Chile, no telling which boat I'll be on later this evening but if you don't see me, you know Sunday dinner is always open. Unless I'm not here, then you have to fend for yourself."

I laid the papers down on the table next to momma and followed Devin to his car. You would think we were in high school all over again the way we both were cheesing. I walked to the car and was happy to see that Devin finally went on ahead and got his birthday gift.

Now we don't have to bum rides from other folks.

Just before we got in the car, I looked at him and gave a smile that only I can give to him.

Seven

I invited Sunni over so we can get dressed and hang out before we hit my all white birthday bash. Since she didn't know many people here, I asked her to hang with me and meet some of my greatest friends. We practically have been hanging out at least once a week ever since she came in the bakery. She seems like she's really cool but I do know people will let their representative show up for them long before you meet the real person. I will say she is spoiled rotten by her daddy riches though.

After coming into the bakery the first time she kept coming in asking did I know where certain places were. I knew she was just as green as the grass itself. I took her under my wing and showed her places she wanted to see. We are totally different when it comes to the men but I don't judge, at least I try not to.

I learned that she has always been a straight A student, graduated with honors, drives a red Mercedes, is sexually active, her momma is not in her life too busy trying to catch another Millionaire husband. It was just her and her dad up until the day he died. Sunni says maybe one-day she will start a clothing line but at this moment she's having too much fun at twenty-one spending daddy Warbuck's dead money.

I already had my clothes hanging up on the back of my bedroom door and Sunni had her clothes draped across my computer chair. From what I can tell through that see through garment bag it don't look like much will be covering her up.

"So Lou girl, let me show you my outfit for tonight; it's bad as hell. Check this out!"

She grabbed the bag and pulled the contents from the bottom of the bag. It had some French name on it that I couldn't even pronounce. When she pulled that dental floss out of the bag all I could do was shake my damn head.

"Where in the hell do you think you wearing that too?"

I just had to ask. I mean the material looked like Freddy Kruger had gotten to it after Edward Scissor Hand had it. Then she was wearing an all-white thong and a jeweled out bra. At that moment, I knew she was an undercover freak. All that shit she be talking about when she's trying to impress someone new, who don't know the things I'm currently finding out about her. That's fine, but here what I'm looking at is something else totally.

"Girl I'm wearing this to the party tonight, shhiidd I'm sure to get some dick tonight in this."

"You got that right. Not one man will be able to keep his eyes off of your ass literally, since it will be out for any and everyone to see."

"I dress like this all the time. When I go out girl, there is nothing like getting the attention of someone's man. Hell because if he looking at my ass then his woman has the problem not me. And I know what the Texas men are working with so now I want to know what the Chicago men are working with."

I couldn't believe half the shit that was coming out of her mouth, all in the short time span we spent getting dressed. I learned more about her sexually than I truly cared to know. I mean don't get me wrong I always hear the freakier you are you have a better chance of keeping your man. Now I don't know how much truth that is since men have a keen sense to hunt for the newest pussy, but it damn sure won't hurt to try. Maybe I can learn something from her that I may not already know. She seems to be very open with her sexuality.

"Hey Lou. That Devin is fine as fuck. Is he seeing anyone? My damn head spent around like the damn exorcist. What the hell she wants to know anything about Devin for?

"Okay Sunni, I see where this is going and let me just say you cool and all but Devin is off limits to you and any of my other friends. No need to ask questions, just please don't cross that line." Sunni looked at me like I had two heads, but I was damn dead serious.

"Well damn. You must got that he just my friend syndrome going on, but if you plan on keeping him in your corner, you're going to have to start acting like you're interested in the man. I mean I never really hear you mention him unless you are telling someone not to go near him, and we all know that shit don't work. Grown folks going to do what grown folks going to do, and at the end of the day, you're the one who is going to be upset. No shade just truth.

I plopped down on my bed and thought about what Sunni was saying. I've spoken to her enough to know that she has been known to have some hidden agendas.

"I hear you loud and clear Sunni. Loud and clear."

Once night fell it was on. I tried to erase what Sunni said earlier but it lingered in the back of my damn head, we both were in the full length mirror trying to get ourselves ready. I rocked some satin booty shorts with a satin and sequence halter top, and of course my strappy white heels. I knew damn well I was looking good. I just wasn't sure what/who I was walking out the door next to. This chick truly looked like she was about to hit the track before and after the club. I mean she wasn't slim with curves like me, she was thicky-thick with curves and to see all that in that cut up ass piece of cloth she had on was more than I care to see.

I looked at the time, took another glance in the mirror, checked my hair and make-up and rolled out. It was damn near nine at night and Devin has already called me three times, most likely wondering where I'm at. I should've been at the club and hour ago; but hell we shutting it down, so it's all good.

"Come on Sunni, it's time for us to hit the club. I'm ready to drink and turn the hell up!"

Sunni grabbed her bag and purse and we both walked to her Mercedes. She threw her bag in the trunk and I jumped in. I dialed Devin back just to see what all the phone calls were for as if I didn't know, after the first ring he answered.

"Where the hell are you Lou?"

"Sunni and I are on our way right now, we will be there in about fifteen minutes. Why are you trippin?"

"Damnit Lou! I'm not tripping but all these hard legs you invited are looking for you and I'm not about to entertain them until Queen Lou arrives. Fuck that!"

"I'll see you soon Devin." I clicked off the phone. Trust me, I knew exactly who was looking for me and so forth. He just mad because I invited so many men.

I wasn't about to start fussing and cussing on the phone. I knew I had already received a few phone calls from a few brothers wondering where I was. So if they want to hang with me they'll be there when I get there; if not they'll simply leave.

"Sunni girl step on it. This fool is clowning hell, he know I got to make sure my shit tight!"

"Shit you don't have to tell me twice, I'm ready to get to this club and get my drink on."

Within fifteen minutes we were parking around the corner from the club. I couldn't believe how fucking crowded the streets were, and it wasn't even midnight. Devin and I closed out the club from all outside folks coming in and partying with our family and friends.

From what I was seeing just from looking out the passenger side window Devin invited quite a few hoochies his damn self. There were a few other cars parking were Sunni and I was parked, and they all had on outfits similar to the shit Sunni had on. Sex was definitely in the air tonight looking at these women but if I know Devin, it's going to be a whole lot of pissed off women leaving tonight.

Sunni and I walked behind the four other women who parked near us. All they kept saying is, "I hope Devin's in here." I shook my head discreetly knowing that if I wanted to dance and drink with Devin all night long, all these half-dressed ass women wouldn't even have a chance.

The music was roaring through the club, you heard it every time the door opened. Something about that Jamaican music makes a woman start whining as she walks down the damn street.

"Girl that music is pumping through them damn speakers. Shit, let's get the hell in here." Sunni ass was more excited than I was but who could blame her. We finally walked into the club and the crowd was in pandemonium when they saw me make my grand entrance. I was bombarded with hugs and kisses and even some ass feels. I was getting drinks thrown in each hand, but all I really wanted to do was hit the dance floor. I don't have much of an ass but what I did have I was going to press all up on whomever was lucky enough to whine with me.

I scanned the room for Devin, when I saw him walking towards me holding two dozen white roses. I felt my face get hot from blushing so damn much. He had a drink in his other hand sipping as he walked towards me. I was in such a shock that I actually stopped hearing the music and focused on his smile. I wanted to take a drink but I couldn't even raise my cup to my mouth I felt paralyzed and not completely sure why I was in such a trance.

He seemed to look better than I have ever seen him before. His white tee, white linen shorts and his white Air Force Ones was making this man look so damn good to me. His smile, his goatee, his hair cut, just everything about him was amplified at this very moment.

When Devin approached me I held my hands out and grabbed the flowers and out of nowhere he kissed me on the mouth, not one of those granny kisses either. It was one of those come here, you're my woman type of kiss. When he pulled away from me I didn't know what to say at that instance; in fact, I was a little dizzy. I looked around and gave my flowers to a friend of mine, I asked her to go put them behind the bar. Devin grabbed me by the hand and I followed like a puppy. We hit the dance floor hard, song after song we bumped and grind, whined, and I got twirled left and right. Shit I've known Devin for a while but dammit, I was shocked to see that he had some serious dance moves. Hell, I was glad as hell because I like to shake my groove thang on the dance floor.

The dance floor was damn near over crowed. Asses on asses, one minute you were dancing with one person and within seconds you were dancing with someone else, except me of course. Devin and I was entangled on the floor, we were actually doing the dance of love. At one point it had to be after the eighth song we grooved to that I had to break and go grab me another Apple Crown on the rocks. I stayed at the bar and mingled with my guest. I glanced over on the floor and saw Devin dry humping on one of the four women that walked in with me and Sunni.

My first instinct was to run over on the dance floor and jump between them but I quickly decided against that. We're here to party, it's a time and place for me to act all jealous; this was not one of them. Time seem like it was going so damn fast, like I didn't have enough hours in the night to dance with everyone I wanted to. I lost Sunni somehow in the crowd but I knew she could handle herself, she was turned up like a motherfucka! I was about to walk away when a strong hand grabbed my arm. I quickly turned around and saw Kevin's ass standing there smiling with red and white roses and a Pandora box in his hand.

I was in total shock, I haven't spoken or seen Kevin since he went overseas to play basketball. My eyes were in shock, my body began to tremble with excitement, and not to mention Kevin was my first sexual experience. I was a junior and he was a senior in high school. When I first saw him, he didn't hesitate to get to know me and I was intrigued. All the girls wanted a senior who played any sport. This man looked good as hell. He sported a short fade, a nice full beard, and had a strong medium build. He looked like he lived at the damn gym.

Kevin and I embraced and I inhaled his cologne, I was in heaven. It was truly awesome to see him. He handed me my flowers and my gift. I asked Terri to hold these behind the bar and Kevin and I immediately hit the dance floor. From what I was seeing all that running around on the basketball court and faking niggas out on the court landed him some great moves on the dance floor.

I rubbed my ass all up on him and just like a pro, he grabbed me around my waist and let me do my thang. I almost felt like we were the only ones on the dance floor. You would've thought that we were having sex on the damn floor right in front of everyone. Now don't get me wrong, I do have a voyeuristic side but this wasn't the place. After a couple songs he went to grab us some drinks and I went to the bathroom. It was a line so damn long, some of the women were going to the men's bathroom. I wasn't in a rush, but damn I didn't want to go to the men's bathroom either. I know that it may not be a pretty sight in there. By the time I finally got in the bathroom the line was damn near gone. The very last stall I never saw anyone go in there or come out, but the door seemed to be closed. I asked a few people was it locked and they just hunched their shoulders.

I hopped out of line and pulled on the door handle. "Who the hell in here? We got to piss out here." My eyes grew big as hell when I saw Sunni and some random coming out of the stall.

"What the hell you doing in here with this dude? And better yet who the hell is he? I watched him adjust his pants as he walked out the bathroom.

"Girl don't trip that's just Jonathan. We danced, had a few drinks and then got horny; this is where we ended up. What the hell is the big damn deal?"

"You're grown. You can do what you want Sunni, but I damn sure didn't think I was hanging out with someone who does random men in bathroom stalls, but clearly that's your get down so enjoy the rest of your night."

I walked my ass to the next stall before anyone else got in there. As bad as I had to piss, someone would have gotten peed on. I came out the stall, washed my hands and checked my make-up. I was still just a flawless as I was when I walked in here. Seems like Sunni was able to fool some folks, but in reality she isn't shit; but a rich thot.

This chick must be losing her damn mind if she thinks I hang with hoes. I don't belong to the birds of a feather flock together group.

Eight

Hands were up in the air ass shaking, titties practically coming out of them little ass tops the women had on. I had a hard on damn near most of the night, off and on that is. I knew damn well Lou ass could move; but damn, she damn near made me want to buss all over her ass, grinding up on me like she my woman and what not. That girl just don't know the kind of mood she puts me in. I've chased her for some time now and when I saw her ass over there at the bar a while ago I knew damn well. Like I had said to myself before, baby girl loves her freedom and I can't trip on that so even though we brought our birthdays in together, I knew it was time I let her go…fuck!

The DJ was on point. I saw some chaos over at the women's bathroom, I didn't pay it no mind. I just didn't want nobody to start acting a damn fool up in here so I quickly turned my attention to a short thick cutie. She was bouncing her ass all over the dance floor. I clapped my hands to the beat of her ass, damn this girl was damn near naked as fuck. I mean all I saw was panties and some kind of blinged out bra. All I can say if I play my shit right, I'll be able to take her down or at the very least she'll take her mouth on a trip down south before I go home and passed the fuck out.

Shorty put on a damn show. We were in the middle of the floor and people gathered around us, watching this chic do the nasty grind on me. I looked to my left and who the hell do I see; Lou ass and some dude who look like he damn near got her in the choke hold and shit. So I went even harder with shorty grabbing all on her ass and titties. I grabbed anywhere she would allow me to grab her and before I knew it, I was still grabbing on her just as we were about to walk out the door. Lou stopped me before I could get out the door good.

"Devin can I holla at you for a moment?" I told shorty with the blinged out bra on to wait for me at the bar while I chopped it up with Lou.

"What's up Lou?" I gave dap and hugs to everyone that was leaving the club. Our time had come to exit the club, it was three in the morning and now I was trying to get out and get in something. And Lou is about to start with some bullshit, I just know it.

"I see you about to step out with ol' girl, but look she ain't shit but a hoe. It's plenty chic's you can get with, but not her. Hoe or no hoe we kind of started a little friendship so please don't cross that bridge." I saw pity in her eyes, she leaned up against the wall and just kept her eyes on me looking for an answer.

"Look Lou, I don't know all about that hoe shit but shorty bad as fuck and I need to fuck, and she is a willing participant. Please don't start tripping on me right now. At this point it's not a good look. And what about ol' boy that had his arms locked on your damn neck?" I know she didn't think I was going to let that shit go, especially since she's over her fucking up my shit.

"First of all that's Kevin from high school. Remember he went overseas to play basketball." Does she really think I remember what the fuck any nigga from high school doing or did.

"Lou this is some bullshit! I don't give to fucks about him. All I care about at this moment is getting back to shorty so I can finish my night and pass the fuck out." I took a deep breath realizing what I had just said. I'm fucked up and I know that shit didn't sound right to me so I know it sounded fucked up to her.

"Fine, I'll let you get back to your night. Be safe Devin." This woman gave me one of the most fucked up good bye hugs ever. Like she would never see me again. What the fuck is wrong with her?

I watched her leave in a red car, couldn't make it out or even who the driver was. At that moment my mind was solely on Lou and not shorty. Even though my mind was on Lou, I turned to see that shorty was gone.

After getting back to my place alone, I had to call shorty and apologize about my conversation with Lou. She seemed to understand and told me there'll be many more chances for us to get together.

Lou ass had fucked off my night. I couldn't believe I let that shit happen. I had a good mind to fuck up her night because if she was with someone, he was going to be one mad motherfucker!

I called twice before this damn woman picked up the damn phone. I guess she did have company over, yup throwing a monkey wrench up in her shit as well.

"Damn girl! Bout time you answered the phone!" I was laid across my bed with my boxers on waiting on her to say something that wouldn't have me cuss her out for the bullshit she pulled tonight.

"What the hell do you want Devin? It's damn near four in the morning, my damn head is spinning and I'm fucked up. I really don't have time for whatever issue we have tonight." This woman must have lost her damn mind if she think I'm letting this shit slide.

"What the hell I want! I know damn well you didn't say that shit to me. What the hell was all of that shit back at the club?" Oh hell no, she's not getting off that damn easy!

"I told you I was done. I was just looking out for a friend that's all, but you were so damn adamant about doing you; so have at it." Here we go with this shit!

"Friend's huh? Don't act like we the kind of friends you pass on the fucking street and keep going. I like to think... no scratch that, I know we're more than that. You're the only one who doesn't see it or you just playing this coy shit." I swear I shouldn't have called her because I feel like I'm getting pissed by the second.

"It's whatever. I guess, ol' girl has cum and gone by now that's the only reason you on the phone with me now. And whatever happens...happen. I told you that she was a whore and a bullshit ass friend by default, and I think that shit just ran in one ear and out the other." I dropped the phone to my side for a brief moment to stop from saying some shit I can't take back. When will she learn?

"Hell if you ever gave me a chance you would know damn well there is no one coming to my house and leaving under thirty, I puts in work my sweet Lou." She going to have me say some shit that'll have her jumping in her car coming to see what I actually do.

"Look I don't want to talk about any of this tonight, call me tomorrow when I feel up to talking."

"Damn, okay Lou."

I hung the damn phone up pissed off. I don't give a shit, that woman know exactly what she be doing and it's my stupid ass fault for letting her do that shit.

I should be in here slapping bellies with shorty right now, but once again I had to listen to all that dumb shit Lou was spitting and let shorty go home. But I do have an invitation to get up with her soon. I think she said her name was Sunni.

Nine

It has been two weeks since we had our birthday bash and I was just having the time of my life meeting new people at the club now since I am old enough to enter them without any bullshit from the rent a cops they had watching the door. Kevin stayed a little longer than he was supposed to for obvious reasons…me. I really enjoyed his company but like most of the guys I run into, not soon after they want to start putting me in the little girl-friend box. Sorry for them; I'm not the one, I'm way too young for that shit.

I'll say as bad as I wanted to sample the goods with Kevin, not really speaking to Devin had my head all over the place. I can't believe he's that pissed off because I tried to warn his ass about Sunni. I mean she was probably going to be a takedown but we had a friendship bonding well at least I thought, and to cross that line would have been just messed up.

I know she's a loose booty. Anyone who gets within two feet of her will know that and the sad part about it is, that she don't try to hide the shit. She tried calling me once since the party and I ignored her ass. I instinctively remember telling her ass not to fuck with Devin on any level. That he was off limits to my friends and close associates. Seems like that fucking memo went right out the window.

I grabbed my keys off the kitchen table as I was finishing my juice before momma came downstairs. Since my momma has turned over everything to me she has been shopping like a mad woman, going to the boat and going out of town. I guess that's what they mean when they say, "paying your dues." I love working at the bakery. Everything I learned, I learned from my momma. No baking classes, no decorating classes, all of it was self-taught. Now I get to bring in some more flavors and I even let the customers come up with their own flavors that we added to the menu.

Sunni texted me and let me know she was going to come to the bakery today to get two dozen pistachio cupcakes. Something tells me this was going to be more than just about cupcakes, especially since I didn't answer or return her call.

I jumped in my car and headed to the bakery and like clockwork I saw Devin and his boys on the court, and as usual the crowd around them started to form. I smiled wishing I was on the court with them, cheering them on but the way our friendship is set up right now, it's best that I keep on rolling; but I did honk my horn for good measure. Pulling up in front of the bakery just moments later, I felt good about having something that belongs to me. I work basically on my own time and to see customers up in here eating tasty treats, reading the latest book, or just catching up with some friends; I knew this was a great place to have.

Not long after I got there, after getting Sunni order together, she was walking through the door. She had about twenty more minutes before her order would be ready so I had to get my mind right to deal with her, and the crazy part is that it's not even twelve yet.

"Hey Lou girl, what's going on with you?" All I could do was, give her a blank ass stare.

"Um, looks like I'm working. I see you are back to your sundress and flip-flops."

"Girl yes, that's just my club attire. Yeah I go from Mary Poppins by day and a Luke dancer by night, and I love every minute of it. If I ever work a day in my life, it'll be because I want to not because I have to."

This girl was rich and delusional. I get we all like money but she can't even be herself without thinking that money makes her. From where I'm standing it looks pretty damn sad to say the least. I informed her that she had a twenty minute wait for her cupcakes and that she could grab a seat, and it had to be one closer to the counter where she could carry on a conversation that was truly not needed.

"So I see you and Devin got some kind of a relationship huh? I mean he couldn't even get out the door good before you were grabbing him all on his arm and shit." Damn she just shocked the hell out of me, no introduction just straight to the point I see.

"We've been friends for a long time. We never dated but we do have each other's best interest at heart. Hurting one of us is like hurting both of us. And whenever I see him making a mistake if it is only for a night, I must speak on it. I mean what kind of friend would I be if I didn't?" I had to let her know real quickly that I don't play them bullshit ass games.

"That's nice to know but trust me you won't be able to stop him the next time he's ready to get with me. I saw you having a little hissy fit so I just left without saying a word but that was only because I knew he would be calling." Why is this woman in here testing my patience?

"Look I thought we were friends or at the very least trying to form one and the type of people I associate with don't sleep with certain men in my life Sunni."

"Lou you just said a whole lot of nothing! See I can understand it if you and him were liking on each other or have had sex or something of that nature but neither one of you are saying anything to that nature. So as far as I am concern he's fair game sugar. I suggest you step your grown woman up and stop all this friend shit if you want to keep him because if not you will lose him." Did she just call me sugar and give me advice on what I should do where Devin is concerned?

"Your order is ready Sunni." I went to the back and grabbed her order. The faster I get her out of here, the better I will feel.

"All I'm saying is don't trip on the next woman who wants the man that you seem to can't even be truthful about. And he seems to keep you in the friend zone as well. We got a cool little friendship but if losing you to get him is what it's going to take; then so be it. I'll have him in the end. In my world, dick trumps friendship any day!" I swear there is no loyalty anymore, now women are only befriending you to get closer to some dude…damn shame.

"Well thanks for that little speech. Let's say we're not friends and you do what you feel you have to do. Enjoy your cupcakes and have a great day Sunni."

I watched her grab her desserts off the counter and walk to the door. As soon as she got to the door she turned and looked at me.

"Sorry it had to be this way Lou, but if you are thinking about calling him and letting him know about our little conversation, remember pussy

trumps friendship."

I knew I was in trouble right then and there.

Ten

Lou ass has been acting real strange for the last couple of weeks and now yesterday she texts me and says, "We need to talk." Like I didn't see her ass the other day honk her horn, as she drove pass the basketball court. If she wanted to talk she should have hit the court. I wanted to bring it up but talking to her at times is like talking to a wall.

I never texted her back. Hell I been trying to catch up with Sunni since I seen her at my party, the girl is damn near impossible to catch up with. I finally took a day off today. Saturdays is always my busiest days but today I just wanted to do nothing especially since I have saved up enough money to go and finally look at my first home. Most would say I'm too young to be buying a home or having my own business, and I say you are never too young or too old to live life the way you see fit.

Living in a studio is cool but it's time to expand a little and I think it'll satisfy the ladies a little more, but I know damn well the size of my apartment isn't the size that's really important.

I sat on my bed listening to the traffic on the street with my window stretched wide trying to get as much air as I could it was a hot ass day not even my fan was doing the trick. Every five minutes it was another car rolling down the street with a different song, hell I had my personal mix going on. I grabbed my phone which was sitting next to me and decided to finally call Lou. I was tired of this cat and mouse shit, and this time I have not one clue what's her problem. I swear if I was going to go through all of these changes, I need to be hitting that at the very least. I placed my head in my hands, and collected my thoughts. Fuck it let me get this shit over with was my only thought.

After the second ring to my surprise she answered.

"Hello."

"Why the hell do you do that?"

"Do what?"

"Say hello when you know damn well it is me calling."

"What the hell do you want me to say?"

"Nothing Lou. I was calling because I got your text. And I need to know what we need to talk about?" She paused for a moment on the phone and this is never a good sign.

"I would like to talk about this later if you don't mind. Come to my house around seven tonight then we can discuss it."

"Okay Lou, I'll be there."

With a one-click motion she was gone. I didn't do anything but look at the phone like some sort of blue smoke was coming through the phone that was about to infect me with a deadly virus. This girl, all I could do was shake my damn head. I wasn't going to be playing this bullshit ass game with her. If we can't be friends, I rather not be nothing. It's not like she breaking a brotha off or nothing.

Ten minutes after I threw my phone on the bed I got a call, shiidd if my face didn't look like a Chester cat, I don't know what it looked like. I pushed the green button and heard this southern accent on the other end asking did I want some company. Before my mouth could say anything my third leg said, hell yes!

Once my mouth caught up with my brain I gave shorty my address and she was on…thee…way! Now most men try and act like they not all excited and shit for a piece of ass, I'm here to tell you that's a damn lie. Especially if it's someone you have had your eye on. There is nothing like a short, thicky-thick, redbone.

I jumped in the shower, threw on some basketball shorts and black wife beater. I was looking good, smelling right so I checked myself in the mirror. Hell I must say twenty-one looks damn good on me. I do know one thing no woman trying to come see a man in the morning unless she wants that good morning sex, it's no different than the midnight creep.

About thirty minutes passed when two taps hit my door. I did a once over through my studio just to make sure nothing was out of place. I didn't even look through the peep hole, it's not like anyone else was coming over this early. When I opened the door there she stood all of 5'4, red bone, cute, and thicker than a snicker. Damn she had such a beautiful smile, just looking at her made my member jump and she looked different too. The way she was dressed at my party screamed back alley whore. But today she has on a casual summer dress and some flip-flops. Real cute, but I thought to myself this must be her day look.

I moved out the way and let her come on in. I can see already that shorty got some games up her sleeve. That just tells me that I have to keep my eye on her if she's going to be around. I get that sense because any woman that dresses like she's about to hit the pole one night, then looking like she on her way to church, then somewhere in the middle lies what she's really about. And to have Lou all pissed off, yeah it's some bullshit in the air and if she's going to stick around, I'll have to get to the bottom of it. But for right now, I know she came to slap bellies and that's what's on the agenda.

"I'm glad you finally used the number, you're one hard woman to catch up with. I began to think you were no longer interested in a brotha." I closed the door behind me and offered her a seat on the sofa. I watched her apple bottom shaped ass get acquainted with the sofa. I was ready to go right then and there but for some reason women feel as if they have to go through the formalities of having a conversation.

"Well I heard from Lou that you were trying to get up with me and to be honest she feel's some type of way about you and me talking and or sleeping together." Sunni placed her purse next to her while she checked the notification her phone had just given her.

Now I'm sitting here wondering what the hell is Lou's problem and when the hell did they get so close where my name comes up in their day-to-day conversations.

"What was said exactly?" I wanted to know. Lou ass always seem like she got an issue with me seeing anyone but she refuse to give me any play. She turned and looked at me, now by this time I am sitting next to her on the sofa.

"To make a long story short she said don't fuck with you because you and her are friends and since she and I were on the verge of becoming friends she didn't hesitate to let me know that I shouldn't cross that line. That's one of the reasons I left the night of the party. I heard everything she said about me and it's cool but whatever kind of friendship we were trying to form is null and void now. "

I was blown away by what I just heard. No wonder Lou been acting all strange and shit. Ever since the night of our party, I knew I should have forced her to say something instead of letting her get away with that little pissy ass attitude she had.

"Okay, let me put this flame out before it gets any bigger. Lou and I are practically best friends. Have I wanted to be with her in the past; yes. Did it happen; no. Now friend or no friend, she damn sure don't dictate who I kick it with. I don't know if that makes a difference to you but to me it's all good on my end."

I was pissed off at Lou. It's just like a female to go and say some shit to the other female because she all in her damn feelings and shit. I bet Lou ass will hear from me later on about this shit.

I heard a car horn blaring outside which knocked me out of my trance of thoughts I was having. I jumped up and looked out the window and it was my boy Terry. He was stopped in the middle of the street when I hung my head out of the window to light weight talk with my homeboy. He flung open the door to his main girlfriends black intrepid. I shook my head only because this nigga is a straight up cock hound and these women still let him drive their whips and anything else he wants.

"What up man! I got another game I'm playing today and we need another player, I know you down."

I couldn't do shit but shake my damn head because if this was any other moment hell yeah I was going to the court but shit I got shorty in here, there is no way in the hell I am going anywhere at this moment.

"I can't today; I got company so I'll have to get back to you later."

By now traffic was starting to pile up behind him, the street was so small there was no way that anyone can get around him. He turned his music up louder to drown out the car horns honking at him, he threw me the peace sign and burned rubber down the block. I knew tomorrow I would have to give him details of shorty but right now, back to business.

I turned and looked at Sunni who was still sitting on the sofa waiting for me to finish my conversation with Terry.

"Sorry about that, my boy wanted me to hang with him at another game today. But I'm hanging with you. It's all about you right now."

She shined that bright pretty smile my way which made me think that if anything was to come from this other than sex it may be a good thing that I was totally up for.

Eleven

It's been two days since I heard from Sunni and I wasn't tripping but dammit the day she came over to my apartment I knew she was going to be special. Everything from a simple kiss to the way she let me hold her was great. When she was there we continued to make small talk which was cool. I could have skipped all of that but I understand that's what women need before they have sex.

While we were talking she leaned over in mid-sentence and kissed me one of those full tongue kisses. She sucking on my tongue I'm sucking on her tongue, I was ready to go. She stood up and lifted her dress up exposing a panty free ass which shocked me but excited me even more. She rubbed her fat ass hairless monkey, turned and placed both knees on the sofa facing the wall and poked her ass out. She didn't say one word. I already knew what time it was, she simply wanted to get fucked.

I dropped my shorts and rubbed the tip of my head against her already moist pussy, giving me more ease to slide ten inches of thick flesh inside of her slowly, as I watched her grip the back of the sofa. I started with a slow stroke feeling her out from the inside then speeded up as her breathing became more erratic, she began to moan softly then moan a little louder. I grabbed her around her thick waist and watched her ass ripple every time I slapped up against her. She bounced her pussy all over my dick until she screamed out she was about to cum, she started shaking and reaching for things that were not there. I dug in her deeper and harder until I reached my point to cum and sprayed her ass cheeks with everything I had to give.

Every time I replay that day in my head and how hard she and I came, I was ready to see her again. But I damn sure wasn't going to call right away, if she wanted to wait then hell we'll wait.

I never got to go see the house that I was supposed to go see but I did reschedule. So after

I get off work then I'm going to see it and hopefully cut a deal. Work was just that; work. It kept me busy and I loved having my own business. If I listen to my father I would never have been in business for myself. I would be sitting in some college class room bored as fuck wasting his money. Like I told him the day I graduated from high school if he wants a doctor in the family he should have another child and place his bets on that child.

As anyone can tell, me and my pops don't have a good relationship, never have. Ever since I was around thirteen when him and moms separated because he was on some drunk shit and he jumped on her. I grabbed my momma's gun and shot that nigga in his leg. He forgave me after he sobered up because he knew he was wrong but I don't even see him the same and from all the yelling and cursing I have heard over the years, I know damn well that wasn't the first time; it was just the first time I was able to do something about it.

My mother stayed with him because she said he was sick and he needed her. Whatever the reason is I simply stay away from him as much as I can. If it wasn't for my momma, I wouldn't see his ass. He wanted to keep me at home dependent on him and his disability check but I honestly believe that he's pissed that my life is so good and his is not. If he clean himself up I may give him a job.

I had four homes that I had to do some yard work for and I was able to do that and make my appointment with ReMax Realty office. I met the realtor over at the house. I was dirty as hell from work but I didn't give a damn, I had on a tank top, jeans and black steel toe work boots. The house was located in the Rogers Park area which is a pretty diverse neighborhood and I would like to raise kids there one day. Don't get me wrong, I love the city of Chicago but I have had to duck down many a day from gun fire so I'll be damn I have to worry about my children when they walking to the store or even to school.

I pulled up to the address. Once parked, I walked up to the house and rang the doorbell. The door flung open and I was face to face with a slim chocolate beauty who had way to much weave in her hair, but she was beautiful none the less. I took a quick glance at her body she didn't have a whole lot of curves but the little she did have was okay as well.

"Welcome my name is Tori Greene. And you must be Devin?"

I walked in the home and felt a sense that this was going to be mines. Just looking at how spacious it was made me smile on the inside. I reached out my hand to shake hers.

"Yes I am Devin."

"Well Devin this is a great home only you and two other people know about this home. The owner wants this house to go to someone who will not only take pride in it but keep it up and love it just as he and his wife did for fifty years. They had no children so they played momma and daddy to family and friends children. Jackson is the name of the owner. Jackson Hart he was a big time Lawyer in his day and his wife was one as well. Their only concern was to help black people stay out of the slavery ship called jail. Once his wife passed away last year he couldn't stand to live in that big home all alone.

A home like this in 2014 will run 300 thousand or more easy, but this man is selling it for 100 thousand. He didn't need the money, he just wanted someone to take care of his home for the next fifty years.

After taking a tour through the four bedroom house I was ready to make a deal but there was no deal to be made. All the owner wanted was for anyone interested to write a simple letter stating why they wanted to live there and that's how the decision would be made.

I wrote my letter with the paper and pen that was provided giving reasons to why I wanted this house. This was a very unconventional way to purchase this home but I didn't care, somehow I knew this house was mine.

Once I left the house I was in my truck replaying what I just heard the realtor tell me. The decision would be made in twenty-four hours. I was excited just thinking if I really got this house and how I would be finished paying for it within ten years or less. I checked the time and it was 7 o'clock at night. The summer air was fucking great. It was the beginning of August which means it was an eighty degree warm night.

I knew at some point I was going have to go see Lou but every damn time I think about doing so I get pissed at her for tripping on Sunni like that. As I rode in the direction of Lou house my phone chimed in and let me know I was receiving a call from Sunni. I had my blue tooth on so I clicked her on.

"Hey Sunni, how are you beautiful?"

"I'm good. Just thinking about you and the other day and wanted to know how do you feel about going out for dinner and drinks with me tonight? Nothing big, maybe some Jamaican food or something."

I was eager to go with her but I damn sure wanted to go home and shower and change first.

"Sunni I'm just leaving work. I need to go home to shower and change first. I could meet you somewhere or I can come and pick you up."

"No, Devin I want to see you just like you are. I want us to be able to see each other in whatever state we are, in at the time and be comfortable with it. If it's alright with you?"

I couldn't do nothing but shake my head. I knew I was dirty from work but damnit I was still good looking so I would pass and anyone who sees me would know that I just got off work.

"Okay sounds good to me. Would you like me to come and pick you up?"

"No I'm already out so I can just meet you there."

"Okay text me the address."

Sunni texted the address she wanted to meet up at, Mr. Brown's. The music was good and the food was good. I've been there a few times. Thirty minutes later I met her there she was already sitting at the bar waiting on me. This time she had on some shorts that came right underneath her ass cheeks, a v-cut black tank top and some heels. I smiled because she did look good but I just couldn't figure her out one minute she dressed like a whore like tonight and the next she dressed like little Miss Sunshine.

We grabbed a table at the front of the restaurant. A sistah came over to take our orders. We both ordered the rum punch and I also had a shot of Hennessy.

"So you like my outfit?"

I didn't know what to say, all it had me thinking about was fucking.

"Honestly it's cool it just has me thinking about fucking."

"Is that so?"

"Yeah it is. First off let me ask you something. One minute you dressed like this and the next you dressed like you going to church. Which one is the real you?"

She turned beet red in the face like she didn't expect me to ask her because I never said she needs to dress that way but I do understand that women who dress like that is searching for attention.

"Well the sundresses are really me when it comes to comfort but when I go out I dress accordingly. It's no big deal."

"I'm going to say this and be done with it. I don't like women who follow the crowd and all that outfit says to me is you want some attention. So if you need more than what's right here in front of you, let me know so I can make sure this shit goes no further."

The waitress brought over our drinks and then took our food orders. I was so damn hungry I could have eaten everything on the menu twice. We both took a few sips of our drinks and I downed my shot of Hennessy. There was a few moments of silence when she broke it.

"Look Devin I really like you and I'm no angel but I can be for the right person. I'm casually seeing someone else. I have only been here a few months but I don't want you thinking that I'm some sort of whore or something."

I think I was still stuck on the part that she is casually dating someone else, I mean it don't bother me, I just don't think I've ever met a women who was willing to come straight out with what she's doing.

"It's cool. I'm not tripping on anything as long as you let a brotha know what time it is.

"Do you?"

"Just remember I don't like women who follow the crowd. If you and I ever be anything other than fuck-buddies you just make sure whatever else you got going on you clean that shit up."

Our food arrived we continued to talk about what it was that we both wanted out of life. From what she tells me, she doesn't have to ever work if she doesn't want to. So now I understand a little bit about her. She is a spoiled brat even at twenty-two. Since her dad died and mom is nowhere around everything she does is for attention. And not to mention when she was in high school she was diagnosed with being a sex addict which lead her to fucking any and everything that crossed her path in Texas and now she making her rounds here in Chicago. The things a motherless child will succumb to.

Twelve

Weeks have gone by and as usual, I work, hang out with my girls and back home. I got a couple of men friends I hang out with but nothing serious. I came and sat out on my porch enjoying the fresh air thinking about the couple of times I've seen Sunni ass. Either it was at my bakery or passing in the streets. She always give me the impression that she knows something that I don't know but what I really want to do is whoop her ass, her devious ass smile makes me cringe.

I hope she never comes back to my shop again, but that's too much like right. She would love to taunt me daily if she could and if she thinks I'm going to be tripping over anything concerning her she is dead damn wrong.

I grabbed my Pepsi off the wooden table that sat next to me while watching everyone on the block just hang out. Nothing special just men kicking it with the women and women acting all coy like they not into whatever the men are whispering in their ear. A car was coming down the street beating hard. My damn windows to my house was shaking, I couldn't make out who it was even though it was only mid- evening. But when it got closer I saw it was a red corvette. Damn it was a beautiful looking car. It had me gawking at it like I wanted a ride then it started to slow down as it was approaching the front of my house. Thank goodness mama is not home she would have come out and embarrassed whoever it is in the car.

When I was finally able to make eye contact with the driver I noticed it was Terry ass.

"Hey what up girl? Why you sitting here all by your- damn- self?" I swear every time I see his ass he in another chicks car. I waved my hand to beckon him to come to me. I wasn't about to move, I was fresh off work and in chill mode. I had on my comfy shorts, tank top, and flip f lops. Terry ass burned rubber while making his way to the corner. All you heard him saying was, "hey baby," seem like to every woman on the block.

"What up Terry? And who fucking car you got this time?" We both laughed at my question.

"Girl you know me. Hell I just turned twenty-two, there is no way I'm trying to settle down so it may be a different chick daily or weekly but believe me, there will be a different chick." We both fell out laughing knowing he wasn't lying.

"I'm just sitting here chilling, just got off work not too long ago. Closed early today which was cool, it was slow anyway. By the way have you seen your boy?"

I just had to throw that in there, I wasn't going to ask but I had to. I haven't heard from him in a couple weeks and seeing him on the court don't count.

"I haven't heard from his ass, other than when we playing ball and usually afterwards he bounce so damn fast we don't have time to chop it up."

I took a swig of my pop and offered Terry one, he declined. I was trying to get my thoughts together thinking what could have him so busy that he's not keeping in contact with no one.

"Do you think he's seeing any one?" When the question left my lips I didn't want to hear the answer.

"Hell, all I can say is if he is seeing anyone, he's definitely keeping this one under wraps." I took more gulps of my damn pop in the last five minutes than I have the entire time it was sitting on the table next to me.

Terry took a seat on the other wooden chair next to me and took a deep breath.

"Man, I fucking love Chicago. There is no other city like it. These thick ass women out here. Thicker the better, the clubs, food I just hope one of these women don't be the death of me one-day."

"Speaking of women, who the hell car is that? Don't act like I didn't ask you that a few minutes ago."

"It's this chick I been diggin out literally; she only been here in Chicago for a few months, hell as of a matter of fact I saw her one-day coming out of your bakery. I was cruising past, we spoke, exchanged numbers and the rest is history."

"Look, don't be soliciting my damn customers Terry."

"Nawl, it's not like that but she cool. She's not Ms. Right for me but she is Ms. Right now, if you know what I mean. As of a matter of fact she was at your party, she was the one wearing a white thong up her ass and a diamond looking bra." Hearing Terry speak about Sunni and smiling through every word made me want to spit fire. Damn! This chick, just wants to run through the crew and what not. I most definitely have to speak to Devin about this, because all the while she trying to get with him, she fucking his boy.

"Oh hell no! You're talking about Sunni ass!"

The look on his face was priceless when I yelled that out. But if I know Terry, no matter what as long as she waxing his knob; he was cool with it. We talked more about Sunni of course, until he had to go and return her damn car. I couldn't believe what I was hearing. I just know one damn thing if Devin has listened to anything I ever had to say I hope he listens now.

Thirteen

I couldn't wait to run my damn mouth. I wanted to call Devin ass so bad but I waited only because I wanted to tell him and sound like an adult and not the kid that was saying, "nah, nah, nah, nah, nah I told you so." Hopefully when I do tell him, he listens real well and don't think that I'm a jealous ass girlfriend who's not a girlfriend.

I knew he would be getting ready for work in a couple of hours and I just didn't want him to go another day thinking that he got an A1 riding with him when he in fact got a zero hoe on his team. Now that I think about it, I should have just given him a chance instead, all we have had were years of Stolen Moments, that really hasn't amounted to anything because I'm playing the field and he's with a hoe. How wrong is this shit? Sometimes you think something may come out of all of those Stolen Moments but it just didn't.

I love me some Devin; always have. But I always felt in my heart of hearts that he wasn't ready to settle down. I mean what young man is? All Devin ever talks about is how he wants a good woman. My thoughts have always been the opposite. I have never thought about having a man and settling so soon was natural. There is a whole damn world out there and I think that in our twenties we should be having a fucking ball; literally. Terry left and I called it a night, eager to speak with Devin tomorrow.

I looked at my phone and realized that time was ticking away once again consumed with my thoughts. I wasn't going to open the shop until noon today so I had plenty of time to go talk to Devin and let him know he needs to consider another option…me.

I quickly hopped out of bed, I didn't even take a shower. I threw on some black lounge pants over my naked ass and didn't even bother to put on a bra; these perky breast was going to be on display today.

I grabbed my keys off of my dresser, slipped on my sandals, ran down the stairs, and out the door before momma could stop me and try filling me up with one of her hearty breakfast. My thoughts was running fast and I couldn't catch up with them. Last night after talking with Terry, I just knew that it was time Devin and I stopped with this cat and mouse game. I didn't have to string him along like I did and trust me I damn sure don't want to settle down right now at least not with anyone other than Devin.

I hopped in the car, started it and as I looked ahead I saw three women standing in the street. If they knew how I was about to punch on the gas they would get the hell out of the way right now. I hooked up my phone so I could listen to my music. I jammed Jill Scott- He Loves Me, all the way to Devin's house which is only seven minutes away. I was just hoping he didn't leave earlier than he usually does. It was only 8 a.m. I swerved through traffic beeping my horn making old ladies jump out of the way. The streets was very calm, only if I didn't have somewhere to be but one more car on the road is more than I need it to be. I was about to call Devin when I realized I was about to make a left hand turn onto his block. I stretched my neck forward looking to see if I saw his car on the street and I saw it parked a little ways down from his apartment.

I pulled right up behind him not caring to park correctly as long as my car wasn't in the middle of the street, I was happy. I shut the car off, hopped out and ran to his door where I pressed heavy on the bell. He lived on the second floor. When I looked up I saw him move the fan out the window so he could look down. I thought he would smile when he saw me but he didn't, he just put the fan back in the window.

I fumbled around with my keys waiting on him to come down and open the door, looking around at the few people that were getting in their cars to go on about their day. Within seconds he appeared with some tools in his hands and walked right pass me to his truck. I was shocked to say the least, I'm the one with the attitude. I couldn't imagine what kind of problem he was having.

"Devin wait a minute! Hold up a sec." I lightly jogged behind him to say what I had to say. Now to find out why did he walk right pass me?

"I see you couldn't find anything else to put on this morning before rushing over here? And why are you over here so early and unannounced none the less?" He finished hauling his stuff in the back of his truck. I knew this was going to be an awkward conversation but fuck it he had to be done.

"I came over here to tell you some really important news that I think you should know. So please don't be trying to treat me like I'm some damn stranger that just showed up on your doorstep begging for a sandwich." Devin took a deep breath and leaned against his truck lacing his fingers in front of him.

"So enlighten me Lou, what the hell is so damn important that you had to just run over here." This is a damn shame but with his bullshit ass attitude I almost didn't want to say anything. I leaned up against the truck with him and prepared to tell him the good news.

"Well I spoke with Terry and he tells me he's seeing that tramp you been trying to hook up with." My heart was doing jumping jacks knowing I wouldn't have to hear about this tramp ever again.

"Is this what the hell you came over here for? To tell me about who is fucking who? I should have known this was some dick and pussy shit. If that was your reason for coming over then I think you need to take your ass back home." He didn't scream, he didn't get loud, he spoke in a low tone that I recognize all too well.

"I just sat here and told you that the whore you been gunning for is fucking your best friend and you mad at me? This is some bullshit!" I was in disbelief. I didn't know whether to keep on talking or walk the fuck away. Before I could actually make my damn mind up; who the hell do I see walking out the front door; Sunni.

"Oh hey Lou what are you doing here?" I could have died two times when I saw Sunni face. I wanted to scream what am I doing here? That question should be the only question being asked right now.

"I came here to deliver some news to my best friend if that's okay with you?"

"Sure sugar any friend of Devin's is a friend of mine. Isn't that right baby?" Sunni then proceeded to kiss Devin's full lips as if she was tasting them for the first time. Devin pulled away from her gently and I felt like a deer caught in head lights just wanting to be hit right at this moment. I wanted to be taken away from the misery I was feeling at this moment.

"Look before y'all get started; yes Sunni any friend of mines is a friend of yours but baby I need to talk to Lou alone briefly before we leave." She kissed him on the lips again and sashayed right in front of me and got in the front seat of his truck. The windows were rolled up but I bet she had her supersonic ears turned up.

Devin and I stood face to face with our arms folded across our chest eyeing each other intently. I couldn't imagine what he was about to say to me that he couldn't say in front of her.

Hell I think it needed to be some shit said in front of her so we can get this shit on and over with, like running her ass up out of here. Damn why is he making this so damn difficult?

"Lou you are a very important person in my life and I don't want to lose you but it's time you stay out of my business especially if you are trying to be messy. First of all, I know all about Terry's ass and he do what he do, which is fuck random women and as far as Sunni goes we didn't know what was going to happen so we just kind of let the chips fall where they may. Yes it has happened pretty damn fast but honestly I just ran out of steam chasing you; you made it painfully obvious that you were not ready for a relationship and that's cool but right now I am."

I swear I saw his mouth moving but the shit that was coming out of it blew my fucking mind. I didn't know how to respond. I didn't know which way to go with this but I couldn't believe it, the one that has chased me is also leaving me.

"Wow when has all this shit been happening and why are you rushing shit with her of all people? Let me guess she must be sucking and fucking the hell out of you. I can't believe this shit. You do remember that you chased me and wanted me? You do remember that we have a solid friendship don't you?"

"Yes Lou. I've never denied any of that. Hell, I just think I said all of that but baby you have worn me out and she seems to want me so that's the route I'm going to take. And so you don't hear it from her or on the streets, I just signed papers to my new home on the North Side of Chicago and Sunni is going to move in with me."

I leaned up against his truck, I felt like my legs were about to give away right from under me. This dude must have lost his damn mind. He can't be this far gone over her in this short amount of time. This shit is just not adding up. I felt the tears swell up in the corners of my eyes but I refuse to let anyone of them fall but they were noticeable. Devin walked closer to me and I stepped back fearing that my tears were going to fall.

"Don't come any closer Devin."

"Come on Lou, don't cry baby."

"This shit that I'm hearing is some straight bullshit. I don't give a damn how you slice it. You know we have always done the cat and mouse thing and now you telling me you are about to play house with this whore. And yes everyone seems to know she's a whore other than you. So do me a favor, go have a nice fucking life, stay the fuck out of mine and the same shit goes for her as well!"

I stormed off starting at a fast paced walk to a light jog, I couldn't wait until I got to my fucking car; I held strong though and kept my tears from falling. I took a quick glance at him and noticed him still standing in the spot I left him in with his arms folded across his chest looking like he was ready to cry.

When I pulled off, I sped right past him not even giving him a second look. My heart was hurting, my heart was in shambles and it was done at the hands of my very best friend.

ONE YEAR LATER…

Time heals all wounds...not!

I haven't spoken to Lou in a fucking year and the shit is still bothering me, every single day. I know Sunni knows that I'm bothered by this but she does keep quiet about it. Don't get me wrong, I love Sunni but I love Lou more, I just couldn't be the puppet she was use to having.

I told that woman time and time again that I wanted her. I don't know if she thought I was playing or what but dammit, I wasn't and I had to move on, she just wasn't having it.

Sure I could have just played the field until Lou got her shit together but all I saw was someone stringing me along and loving every minute of it. I personally don't think Lou was going to give me a chance anytime soon. She had already said that she was not ready to settle down and actually I really wasn't ready either but in a fucked up way I wanted to let her know that I can move on without her.

My house is wonderful. Sunni has decorated it. I just wanted a nice home to live in but she did put her womanly touches on it and made it even better. Sunni is a bright woman but I knew we would bump heads a lot if she didn't change. She act as if hanging out every night is the thing to do. I think in your twenties yes you should be out beating up the streets and anything else you can beat up. But with the things I'm striving for in my life, putting in work for my growing business and my home is at the top of the list for me; everything else was secondary.

All Sunni wanted to do was spend money and she had a lot of it which was good she spent her money on all the bullshit she wanted and I took care of my house. She didn't even want her name on the house, which was strange when that conversation came up because that shit wasn't happening anyway. She always said that, only women who want their name on a house is a woman who eventually wanted the house. It all sounded like some bullshit but I didn't care, because if she ever wanted to bounce, she could do that with my house intact.

Sunni was already talking about kids and I wasn't even thinking about kids. Yes I was pounding that ass every chance I got but no, I didn't want kids right now and I made that shit plain. She shopped and I worked, it worked out but don't get me wrong she did give my life something that I didn't have. Hell, maybe I'm burnt already at age 22. Yeah it sounds crazy I know but true. I took down as many women as I possibly could all through high school.

Every man wants one woman, even young ones. Hell, my parents got married when they were in their early twenties but that is also why they were miserable.

Most nights when I get home I usually walk two blocks to the beach just to clear my mind. I'm cool with Sunni for now but I don't know what the future holds and I'm in no rush. But like everything I do we're just going to see what happens. I know like so many women she does has whore like tendencies. I'm cool with that as long as it's in the bedroom but I know damn well she be acting buck when she go out with her home-girls. When I feel like she doing that I call my homeboys and bounce. Hell, night life in Chicago is the right life.

Any club you go in is wall to wall women, not a one I want to take home but certainly some I wanted and did fuck. Hell, I knew Sunni wasn't faithful but I just blamed it on our ages and the fact that she got that sex addiction thing going on.

I wanted to prove to my pops that I can own my own business and buy my own damn house without his help... I did that!

I don't know what the future holds but I'm not going to keep dwelling on the past. Lou and I have had out time and we didn't move on it. I think sometimes I just should have waited but if she wanted me, she would have given herself to me. Sometimes I think people are not always meant to be in a relationship sometimes you get people as friends and that's it. Maybe Lou was only meant to be my friend.

I don't even see her coming to the court anymore. The only thing that's lets me know that she's okay is when I drive past her bakery and I see her beautiful smile shine as she speaks to a customer. I have spoken with Lou's mom only because she has always treated me like a son. She said that she was disappointed that I've stopped coming around and she understood why but she wanted to make sure I was okay. Which I'm not but I am maintaining. I often think that my decision to live with Sunni may have been an impulse decision but the look on Lou's face when I told her about it broke me down.

There are some women that come in your life that you never hurt and then there are some women that you simply don't give a fuck about, and I've not given a fuck about a lot of chicks. Lou wasn't one of them.

I need to focus more on Sunni and less on Lou. It was my decision to leave the way I did, it was my decision to say what I said so there really is no need to keep rehashing the same old shit. But Sunni is not stupid, she knows what I feel for Lou, but just like a woman she used her womanly assets to push Lou out and it worked.

Like now I'm sitting on my deck just people watching, rolling a blunt. I check the time on my iPhone and its noon and I have no idea where

Sunni is. She left here early this morning saying she was going to go and visit her father's grave. I guess that's her story and she sticking to it. I just wish she was more original with her shit.

I heard a car horn honk as it turned down the alley. Since my deck is in the back of the house, the front of the house is on a busy street so many of my neighbors and I sit on the back, either on the porch or our decks and watch each other do whatever it is we doing. Harmless but you do find out a lot about people just by watching them. Just like the woman who just honked her horn at me, man she is definitely a plus size diva and I would tap everything on her, but she is messy as hell. And if I break her off some of this dick, I know for a fucking fact it'll be on the front page of the Sun Times newspaper by morning.

I took another pull on my blunt just when I got a beep from my phone alerting me I had a text message. I usually don't answer text messages right away because I feel if you really wanted me you would call. But I took a look at the text anyway.

Hey babe, I am on my way home. Picking us up some lunch, see you soon xoxoxo.

I laughed at her text and didn't think of texting her back. She knew she had been gone way too long because we both know she was

not at her father's grave site.

But it is cool as long as we both know what the

truth is we don't even need to speak on it. I'll

just finish off my blunt until she brings the jerk

chicken and whatever else she decides to bring

with it, and fuck the shit out of her like she is

being the best woman in the world.

He was a friend of mine

Wow, a whole damn year has passed and I am back at the end of another summer. I actually spent my twenty-second birthday at home, a few friends came over and kicked it with me, momma gave me some money as usual and went on off to the casino for a two days. I tell you that woman will live in the casino if you let her. Terry brought his fine ass over at 2 a.m. trying to get some ass and I will not lie, I wanted to give it to him like I have ever since I found out that Sunni nor Devin thought I was good enough of a friend to not hook up.

I knew if I crossed that line, I knew damn well I couldn't come back from that so I do entertain him but not on a sexual level…at least not yet.

Devin's words hit me like a fucking bull dozer the day he told me about him and Sunni. I couldn't believe the shit that was coming out of his mouth especially since I was going to get my man finally…or so I thought.

I have thought long and hard about what happened and why it happened. As much as he wanted me all of a sudden he falls inside her pussy and wants nothing to do with me anymore. Bullshit! He has said it out of his own damn mouth that he would wait for me but it is mighty damn funny how she moves her ass here and he gets with her and in mere months, she's now moving in with him. That makes no fucking sense to me.

I did speak to my mom and asked her advice about why did things go the way they went? Momma was always clear cut and straight to the point about anything I ever asked her. I knew I wouldn't like what she had to say but I asked, so I had to listen. She looked at me and spoke these words just as soft as the clouds move across the sky.

"Baby no man on this earth wants to be let down by a woman who he has chased for some time. When a man is choosing you that's a clear indication that he is thinking long term if he is true to his feelings. But you let him down Lou, and even though you both are extremely young Devin is just one of those young men that knows exactly what he wants and when. He was simply tired of the cat and mouse game. Even though in my heart of hearts I believe he moved to fast with that Sunni girl, it's truly to try and get over you. He has an old soul at some point this will be fixed. None of this can be easy for him either so if you are going to be hard on him for choosing her, be just as hard on yourself for not choosing him".

I will not lie that last part my mom hit me with stung like hell! Why can't everyone see that two young twenty-two year olds, do not need to be trying to settle down and even though we just turned twenty-two it still applies. I mean most people in their twenties are running around trying to sleep with everything that is not nailed down and I don't understand any of this. All I ever wanted was to have as much fun exploring then maybe around my late twenties early thirties Devin and I could finally make it official but he seem like he's in a race that he is running all by himself. Trust me no one was trying to run that marathon with him. Hell, his own friend slept with Sunni, so like I said people in their twenties are trying to sleep with anything that is not nailed down. I honestly don't know if

I ever want to speak or see him again. I believe he choose pussy over me point, blank, period.

I have avoided him at all cost and I refuse to pick up a phone or anything. He showed his weak side and I don't give a damn, no one wants to be in a relationship that damn bad that he gets with and move a chick in with you so damn fast. Maybe one day he will tell me the real reason why he just had to have her? Why he just didn't wait for me? Why is it so important for him to settle down now? There is some questions that need to be addressed.

I would have never thought in a million years that I would not be speaking to Devin ass. I believe he let a woman come in between us, he may not see it but I know for a fact that, Sunni

ass fucked and sucked him into submission, and

like a man thinking with his dick he went

running like a little ass puppy.

No matter how much I try not to think of him

he does creep back into my thoughts. I often

think about the time when we almost had sex at

my house. I was ready, he was ready but like

always we had another Stolen Moment.

Momma always said she thought we were made

for each other. Hell, I guess momma was wrong

on this one. And to think he hadn't even

attempted to call, text or nothing. He still plays

ball on the court but I refuse to take my ass on

the court and speak to him. He has shown that

he can do without me and I damn sure will do without him.

Don't get me wrong, I miss him like crazy. The joking, laughing, sharing stories, and secrets. But he crossed the line when he knows damn well he shouldn't have. He could have possibly messed around with any other female and I would have light weight been upset but that was our get down. Our friends was always off limits. He feels like just because I didn't know her for a long time then there should have not been an issue.

I say to that…FUCK THAT! Maybe we can hash out our issues but for right now he can kiss my ass, and he and Sunni can live happily ever after.

There's a new sheriff in town

Neither one of them have a fucking clue on what I can control. First let me explain. Devin is a man, throw some pussy his way and he will submit. If only to fuck; he will submit. And poor little Lou, she thought that little song and dance she was doing with him all this time was going to last. Hell, I don't know any man who will keep sitting around a woman getting blue balls on purpose. When my daddy died I decided to move here; I needed a fresh start. No one knew me except for a few people I've met along the way by hitting up secret hotel sex parties. Just like in Texas, I did what and who I wanted no questions asked, and the same thing applies here. I made Devin a game. I wanted to see who would bed him first, me or Lou. She was so hung up on doing things her way, that's when I knew she was going to lose her precious Devin.

If you get a man and you put your best sex game down on him, and make him think you're going to be the best thing he's ever had in his life; then you got him. I watched Lou and Devin do their thing as so called friends. He seemed as if he had started giving up on the possibility of being with her on any level. Let the truth be told, I do love Devin but I am not in love with him. I just did what I did to get him because after Lou tried to jump hard, I knew I had to do something to teach her ass a lesson. I did tell her pussy trumps friendship; I guess she thought I was lying.

I don't think I have it in me to be a faithful woman to anyone. Not only because I'm in my early twenties; but I simply love variety. After telling Devin that I'm a sex addict, I found no reason to keep lying to him. We have a, don't ask don't tell policy. I found out real early in life that I was one. Before my mom ran off to find her next millionaire when I was in high school, she took me to the doctor because she began to notice that I hung around boys a lot. She caught me having sex in the house more than once. I've had porn on my lap top and she just strolled her nosey ass in, and caught me watching it.

She thought I had some kind of mental problem but when the doctors asked me a series of questions, they found out that I had slept with the entire football team at my high school back in Texas. I was then diagnosed with being a sex addict. I couldn't have been happier only because I had something to blame it on. It was a go for me, my mom just brushed it off, but we kept it from my dad. His only job was to make the money so we could spend it; it's not like he would have cared to hear it anyway.

Once Devin and I moved into our new home don't get me wrong, I was shocked that he wanted me to live with him. I knew we had a great sex life and we had sex every chance we got, but I didn't think he was making plans for us. He was making plans for himself and I just happen to fit into his plans to piss off Lou. When he asked me to move in with him I eagerly said yes. I didn't ask no questions. I just knew we were about to make it official. We made the move to the house he already had picked for himself. All I could think about was should I use my money and get a bigger house, but I learned a long time ago from my momma that you can catch more bees with honey than you can with vinegar. So I let him lead. I followed and kept doing what I wanted. Why? Because I kept him happy so I thought and he kept me happy so he thought, and the whole time I was sexing other people and I know damn well he was fantasizing about Lou.

I see that this is going to be quite interesting, for as long as we can keep up this charade of a perfect relationship, which is far from perfect. Devin is always looking at me like I have stolen his best friend. I say to that, if you truly wanted anything to do with Lou his ass should've just played the field like the rest of us until that little red rooster came home.

Yeah a few times I talked about marriage and babies, and that's only because I knew damn well he would pretty much agree to anything I asked at this point, so I may test him and see how far this goes. He's so hell bent on proving a point to Lou that he's willing to do anything. Whatever he decides to do with his life is his business but I'm not nor will I give up my home just because I live with him now. My home is where I get to do all the things that I want to do. I have full out orgies, swinger parties, anything that I want to do that Devin is not a part of.

I'm sure he knows I'm not faithful, but who cares. He knew I wasn't faithful when we first got together. I told him about me sleeping with his friend Terry. That was just not a big deal for me, it's only sex. I love sex and no matter how often I have it with Devin, it's still is not enough. I crave sex, I think about it when I'm sleeping, sex has had me leaving my bed at two in the morning just to go to my house and have a man fuck me in the ass. That's just how important it is to me and my only problem is, that people will soon find out just how much I need sex and start judging me.

Not that I really care but this is a true illness that I have, and there's not enough pills in this world that can cure it. Only having my way with a man or woman is going to be satisfactory. I still haven't gotten to the point where I want to introduce having a threesome to Devin. He says that he would love two bomb ass women on his dick but he hasn't pushed the issue. That further lets me know that he's not into the things that I'm into, and that's okay as long as he knows that I'm going to indulge whenever and however I see fit.

I bet one damn thing, I bet Lou ass isn't and can't fuck him in every way possible. How I know this is simple. Any woman who is loving a man like she claims to be will be willing to do any and everything to him and for him. As for me this is my natural get down, no extras or anything. Hell I would fuck a man until he became blind if I fucked him with extras, but I do know that most women need extras and then you have those like me that don't need shit but their bomb ass sex game. Whoever said the way to a man's heart is through his stomach lied like a motherfucker. The way to a man's heart is simply through his dick. Now that's not to say that he won't cheat but dammit you can rest assure that he's not going anywhere.

I always felt like the sooner women understand that men like to fuck the better they'd be. They are visual people. The first thing a man is thinking about when he is speaking to a woman is sex and it is nothing wrong with that, but so many women try to manipulate the issue. There are just as many women thinking about fucking and sucking a man as there is men thinking about fucking and sucking a woman. Men are just more honest when it comes to that topic. Women on the other hand want a man to feel like there is no way on God's green earth that they are thinking about fucking

simply off of sight. Bullshit!

Until women start owning up to the reasons

on why their pussies are staying wet then I will

keep the torch burning, because I'm not

switching up a damn thing. If I'm not your cup

of tea, move the fuck around. And if I'm come

on and take a few sips. I guarantee you will love

it.

Lying to myself

A whole fucking year has passed and the only thing about Sunni I love is her good looks and her sex; nothing else. Trying to make a point has caused a real bad situation between me and Lou and I need to change all of this. I don't know if she wants to talk to me. I really don't know but I do know that the time has come for use to mend these broken hearts. I know like a motherfucker that I hurt her and I was hurt my damn self.

I mean damn, I have chased this woman all through high school and still even now, and it seems like she was having just as much sex as I was having. I knew she wasn't looking to be mines and only mines. I could have smashed Lou a thousand times over, but then what? She and I would have been at each other's throats daily, based off the fact that I gave her the DICK! I don't give a shit what women say, once you put some back breaking dick up in them; women lose their fucking minds, and that shit goes for men too. Let a woman take care of the dick like no other, we have a tendency to lose our minds as well. We just have a better way of concealing it.

Don't get me wrong, I have wanted to fuck the life out of Lou ass for some time now but I truly, believe us never taking that to the next level is a really good thing. I know for damn sure she would have lost her mind.

Sitting here on my deck, of course Sunni is gone and I really don't give a fuck; it will be nice if she stays out all night long. I rolled me a blunt and see Tasha across the way with the shortest shorts and smallest tank top I have ever seen. I know one damn thing, if she sneeze her ass and her titties will be on display for the whole damn neighborhood to see. The night air is hot as hell. Unless you have air condition, there's no way you would want to even sit in the house.

I'm sitting here on the back enjoying my blunt, listening to the traffic from the front and now this tramp wants to come across the alley way and flaunt her little curvy body in front of me like I truly give a fuck. Hell, I can get pussy any day or night, and what the fuck would I want with this chick. Hell I've already fucked around and got a whore in my fucking house; it's not like I need two of them in the damn house.

My life right now could possibly belong to a forty year old man who has played enough that all he wants to do is settle down. I want to settle down or at the very least know that I have one woman that I can call my own. Hell, I will not lie to myself, I love fucking raw. I love doing all kind of nasty shit, but we all know that's not possible when you are fucking random women. Trust me I am not trying to catch nothing that I can't get rid of, that's for damn sure. At some point I'm going to have to be real with myself and Lou, and anyone else for that matter, and let that woman know that everything I have done up until now concerning Sunni was to simply piss her off, and shit has gotten out of hand.

The sad thing about Sunni though, she thinks I don't have a fucking clue about her late night fuck sessions at her old house. I wish she would simply pack up her shit and go back over there, that way I can go back to my life with a clear conscience. I think I have gotten high enough where I should text Lou after all this time. Will she text me back, I don't know. But dammit I'm tired of playing these bullshit ass games. I'm restless; I need to be with the one who has had my heart all this time and stop playing with people's feelings.

No, no, no why the fuck is she coming over here? "Hey Devin, you can smell that fire all the way over on my deck. I know you don't mind sharing?" I knew this shit was going to happen. Next time I'll smoke my shit in the house. "No I don't mind sharing. But I don't have any more blunts." Hopefully that'll stop her ass. "No worries Devin, I have two in the house. Let me grab the blunts and I'll be right over." I knew I had some on lookers trying to figure out if I'm about to smash or what. I know all too well the few females that wouldn't mind having something to report back to Sunni in hopes that I'll fuck with them. If it's one thing I can't stand, that's a messy ass female.

In mere minutes I saw Tasha bring her ass back across the alley way with what looks like she has a bottle of liquor in her left hand. "I thought we could sip on this while we blaze." Tasha smile was wide as all outside. She held up a bottle of 1800 Silver. I didn't disagree to it, I just wanted my night to be drama and bitch free. "Yeah you brought that shit right on time Tasha." I pulled out the chair next to me so she could have a seat. Tasha passed the blunts to me. "We need some cups." Tasha said that with a look of pure evil in her eyes. Her lips said we need some cups, her eyes said I'll go in the house. You follow and come fuck me into a coma. I wasn't playing no games with this woman. "I'll go get them. Hang tight." I ran in and grabbed two red cups from the counter.

Tasha and I sat out drinking and blazing. I pretended to listen while she talked about her no good ass boyfriend who she cheats on every chance she gets. And the sad part about it is, she think she got one up on him. "Why do y'all women do that dumb shit?" She looked at me like I was speaking Swahili or something. "What dumb shit are you talking about Devin?"

"Clearly I'm talking about why the fuck do y'all start putting y'all pussy on display for all the other niggas just because yo' nigga fucking up? I mean honestly, the niggas you giving it away to, to piss your man off don't respect you and trust me, the man you laying up with at night don't respect you, that's why he's doing what he's doing. And somehow, you think fucking other niggas is going to get him to act right. Take it from a man Tash, once you start fucking other men, the man you thought you had, will never be yours again." Women need to really start taking advice from men. I see the shit happen all day every day and I am no exception. Sunni has long fucked up any possibilities of us actually being together. Then she has the nerve to want a baby. Shit not in this life with this dick.

Tasha and I passed the Sour Diesel Kush back and forth, refilling our red cups until we both were seeing the bottom of the bottle. I must admit looking over at Tash in those short ass shorts and little ass shirt definitely isn't looking so damn bad right about now.

"So what am I supposed to do? Just let this nigga think he can play me and get away with?"

I start sensing her, *I'm a woman about to explode attitude.* I had to do something to defuse this shit immediately.

"No. What I'm saying is, if you know his ass is fucking up then act like you know you deserve better. Even if that means putting that nigga out. But under no circumstances are you supposed to go fucking other niggas to prove a damn point. Once that happens, y'all women have just given us the upper hand. And y'all say we think with our dicks. As far as I'm concerned, all of the women that I've come across think with their pussy and be making bad choice after bad choice." I was just about to swallow the last of my drink when she through some shit in the mix.

"So if you knew your girl was hosting an orgy party right now, you wouldn't be pissed?" How the fuck did we just get on my girl and orgies?

"Trust me, if my girl was having orgy parties, I would know all about it."

"Is that right." I knew she was trying to set her bait at this point. I looked at Tash, soon after I drunk the last of my drink.

"Let me save you some time sweetheart. I know Sunni have all sorts of sex parties at her other home and I could care fucking less." Tash fired up our second blunt, my third before she spoke.

"Well what you didn't know is, she is with my play cousin Terry right now; possibly with his dick in her mouth." All I could do was shake my head at her little comment. That didn't shake me either way. I pulled out my cell phone opened my text messages and let Tash read the one from Terry.

What up my nigg. Hey your girl invited me to an orgy party. Just wanted you to know. You know my get down.

"Make sure you read my response to him before you give me back my phone."

You already know what it is my nigg. Make sure you fuck her good so she won't be expecting me to fuck her later.

"This is some bullshit! You don't care if another nigga is fucking your woman?" I laughed out loud because I don't think she heard me earlier.

"It's like I said earlier Tash, once you start fucking other men, the man you thought you had is no longer yours anymore. I say it all the time, women have to start thinking with their heads and not that fat clit that keep y'all so damn riled up." As soon as my words left my fucking mouth, my eyes looked down at her fist sized pussy that was sitting inside them little ass shorts. This little ass cut off red tank top she had on, that was virtually see through had her marble sized nipples on display the entire night. Now as a man who wants to fuck and I do mean fuck right now. I wanted to take her in the house and fuck her brains out, but I knew better than to fuck her in my house.

"Look it's no need to talk about Sunni or any other woman for that matter. I think I have schooled you on the basics enough for the night." I checked the time on my phone and I couldn't believe it was after two in the morning. Sunni usually gets in around five.

"Damn I didn't realize it was so damn late. You need to walk me to my door. It's late as fuck out here." Once she stood up I saw her trying to adjust her shorts but to no avail, those motherfuckas were not moving. Those motherfuckas was stuck right where they were, all up her ass. She pretended to yawn and stretch her arms as high above her head as possible. She knew damn well those dark circle areolas and fat ass nipples was going to greet me. I smiled at her attempt to seduce me.

"Yeah I got you. Let me pull my damn door up first." She started walking to the back gate. Once across the alley, we walked through her gate and up a few stairs where we stood on her back porch. She was fucked up. She was slurring her words and shit, leaning forwards and backwards I was faded my damn self but not like her.

Once she finally got her door opened after trying three wrong keys I walked inside her apartment with her. "Do you want me to cut on some lights so you can see where you're going?" I couldn't see shit in this dark ass apartment and she was fucked up, so I just knew she thought the kitchen was a bedroom.

"Negro please, this my house. Fucked up or not, I know how to get around in the dark up in here. But I do have to go to the bathroom though. Wait right here until I come out." I know she was staggering because it sounded as if she was bumping up against the damn walls as she walked. I sat down in one of her kitchen chairs. There was a little light shining inside the kitchen from the outside street light. Which at least let me see a little bit.

"Are you still here?" Tash came out the bathroom immediately looking for me. I started not to say nothing and have her thinking that I had left.

"Yeah. Sitting in the same dark spot you left me in."

"Well hell. I had to go to the bathroom. You could've went to the living room and sat." Before I could respond letting her know she asked me to stay right where I was. I felt her warm soft body lean up against my face.

She grabbed my hands and rubbed them all over her naked body. I kissed her midsection, turned her around and kissed each ass cheek. I wanted some more light. I wanted to see those fat nipples and fat pussy and not just feel around on them in the dark. "Baby let take this to the bedroom where I can see all of this body of yours in better light."

We stumbled to the bedroom. Once there, she cut on the light and dimmed it. The room was lit like it was under a candles spell.

"Lay back on the bed." Tash laid on the bed I dropped my jeans and boxers, and black wife beater. The whole time she started masturbating, damn her body was beautiful. I got up closer and was taken back a little by her extremely large clit. If I didn't know any better I would have to say it was a miniature dick.

"Yeah I get that reaction a lot." She saw the look on my face her clit was about an inch long if I had to guess. Her pussy was perfectly shaven, big clit or not I was ready to taste her. I knelt down in front of her and inhaled her womanly scent. That pussy was strong like musk oil, letting me know it was ready.

After a few licks and hard sucks on her clit, she was spraying my face with her juices; my dick was harder than penitentiary steel. I pulled her to the edge of the bed, wrapped her legs around my waist and slid deep inside her. I heard her gasp when I felt my balls lay up against her ass. "Yes baby keep that dick deep inside me." I watched her push her breast together and suck on each of her nipples. Damn that shit was sexy. "Don't worry baby, this dick will stay deep in this pussy." I fucked her long and hard, then switched it up and fucked her long and soft. I've heard about women squirting, but damn this woman's faucet was turned on high with no way of cutting it off. She squirted so damn much that shit was turning me on more and more until I felt myself about to cum. "Damn Tash I'm about to cum. Damn this pussy good."

"Wait baby let me swallow all of you." I pulled my dick out, watched her sit up on her knees and take all of my dick inside her mouth. She used no hands, just all mouth and neck. In mere minutes I grabbed the back of her head and exploded all in her mouth. I painted her tongue creamy white.

I stumbled backwards and leaned up against the wall. My knees felt weak as fuck. Tash laid back on the bed and wiped her mouth with the back of her hand then her top blanket. I got dressed, kissed her on her forehead and headed

out the same way I headed in.

Easy go easy come

I couldn't believe the shit that was coming though my damn phone. A week ago I was hanging out with a on again off again friend-with- benefits, named Charles. He used to come to the court and watch the games and sometimes we would go together. That was the same night that Devin came over and asked me was I sleeping with Charles. It didn't matter then and as far as I'm concerned it damn sure don't matter now. Charles and I were just hanging out after leaving the bowling alley playing midnight bowl. We stopped off at one of the many twenty-four hour greasy spoon joints to soak up some of that damn liquor we smuggled inside the bowling alley.

I was sitting there enjoying a hot cheesy beef with peppers when I looked down at my phone after feeling the vibration on my thigh.

I miss you Lou. I know I fucked up and should have never let Sunni move in with me. Please Lou can we talk.

I looked down at my phone and damn near choked on my damn food, the look on my face must've been priceless because Charles got all up in my business.

"Is everything okay? You look like you just got a message from the dead." As far as I was concerned, it might as well have been. I didn't have anything to hide from Charles. We have an open door policy, we tell each other everything.

"That was that dude Devin I have told you. After a whole year he has decided to reach out to me through a damn text." I slid my phone between my thighs as I tried to continue to eat my food.

"Look Lou stop saying, "dude." As much as you have told me about him, I know he is not just some dude. Maybe he's trying to make things right between y'all again. Haven't you punished him long enough?

"Devin had long enough to make this right."

"Says who? You. Just because he didn't move at the speed you wanted him to move, don't mean he isn't trying. See it for what it is Lou and not for what is was." I squinted my eyes at him, wishing like hell he wasn't making any sense right now.

"Don't be throwing all that logic shit my way Charles. I don't want to hear it right now."

"I know you don't. You really want a reason to sit here with your lips poked out and conjure up an attitude. So everything you do you will feel justified in doing so." Damn! I hate when Charles ass start talking from the book of logic. I took another bite of my sandwich and listened to what Charles had to say.

I've been contemplating texting him back over this last week and I haven't made that text yet. I really don't know what to say except to scream down on him and I don't even want to start off with that shit. I just know that I have to be careful on what I say to him especially since I'm still pissed off with him for choosing her over me, and letting a whole damn year pass.

I know things ended badly between us, the day I jumped into my car and left him standing next to his. I know men do some stupid shit and that was some stupid shit on his part, but to have a woman feel like she got one up on you is the worst pain any woman can experience from a situation like this. I know Sunni felt like she was in my spot, the spot that Devin was supposed to be saving for me. Like any man with a brain Ms. Sunni has to know that no man on god's green earth will wife a whore. Hell that's a thumb of rule from the men's handbook. She's what my mom would call a good time girl, nothing more nothing less.

I have seen Sunni from time to time in local places. We don't acknowledge each other and that's just how I want to keep it. She usually give her fake and phony smile, that's something she can always keep. Her day is numbered in Devin's life and just in case I didn't know better, his text tells me so. Momma always says you have to let a man sort out his own bullshit before he can ever make it right with you, and my response to that is if he hadn't cross the line there would be no bullshit for him to sort out. But that's momma's advice, not mine. I think I'm going to let Devin sweat a little while longer. This is not a game. I just want him to know that it's some folks that you play and it's some that you don't, and I'm definitely in the some that you don't category. Maybe if I entertain Charles a little while longer these days I can get my mind off Devin and Sunni ass.

Finally I'm done

I haven't seen Devin ass all fucking day, I know he had to work but damn he left out at seven this morning. I need to talk to him and I need to talk to him now! I was losing my mind ever since the day I had an orgy party at my house, we haven't really said two words to each other and that was a month ago. I asked him is anything wrong, he says he's cool, but I know he lying. I swear if I find out that fucking Lou is trying to creep her ass back into his life, we're going to have major problems.

I checked my phone and saw I had two missed calls from Terry and Charles, I was not interested in talking to neither one of them at the very moment. I paced back and forth in the kitchen feeling extremely ambiguous. The choices that I have to make will not be an easy one. After grabbing a glass for some apple juice I sat down feeling light headed and somewhat dizzy. Resting my head in the palm of my right hand, I took a couple of deep breaths trying to regain my composure.

It was now after seven at night and still no Devin. I called him, no answer and the same thing with the texts. I don't know what kind of game he's playing but this shit is ridiculous. I was able to pour my juice and sip on it a little bit, I decided to go lay on the sofa. The house was comfortable and cool, the temperature outside according to the news was hitting the high 80's. Thank goodness I have the cool lake breeze just in case I wanted to go sit out on the deck. While resting on the sofa I pulled out my cell phone and called Terry ass back. I know he don't want shit but some ass anyway. After the third ring he picked up the phone.

"What up Sunni?"

"Nothing not feeling too well right now, but I'm just returning your call."

"Oh I didn't want nothing major. Seeing if you got plans at the house tonight?" See I knew he was up to trying to get some ass.

"Not tonight. I told you I wasn't feeling well, so I'm just going to chill at the house tonight."

"Alright ma, feel better and get at me when you do."

The phone clicked off and I waited about five minutes before calling Charles. He's another one who don't want nothing but some ass. The phone rung four times before I was about to hang up then I heard his deep melodic voice almost about to Barry White me up out of my panties.

"Hey Sunni. I haven't heard from you in a few days, how's everything going?"

"I'm cool. I haven't been feeling well for a few days so I'm resting, but I did want to return your call before I settled in for the night." Charles was one of the first men I met when I moved here and he has been a great friend with benefits.

"I hope my pretty lady feels better soon because I would love to see you again." No sooner than he said that my brain thought the same thing.

"As soon as I'm up to par I'll call you so I can come and lay under you or you under me, whichever comes first." We said our good byes and good nights. I swear it's something about dealing with Lou men that keeps me hungry for more. Or maybe if she wasn't always playing that he such a friend role I wouldn't bother, but because I know it will bother her at some point, I fuck them and don't see nothing that's going to change it. If she stop playing and start fucking and staying, she wouldn't have this problem.

Everyone that I did know, wanted to know how I feel getting done by men and women. My response to that was, just as good as you feel when you fucking whomever it is you want to fuck. Back in Texas I knew that the boys were no match for my sexual appetite and there were plenty teachers that were. They tried to pay me off to keep quiet but that was not what I needed.

I didn't need the money. Hell my daddy was rich but I knew they needed to give me something other than their Viagra dick to keep me quiet. I was cool with it. I just wanted to make sure I got all A's, every report card.

The women that were bi-curious, I just say they wanted a lick-her-license, and needed someone they could lick without telling their business; I fit the description.

My first encounter was in my junior year. I have watched so much lesbian porn that just the mere thought of having a woman do me better than any man I had ran across, would simply blew my fucking mind. While in gym class all the girls wore short shorts and even though we were sixteen and seventeen most was already showing signs of having a fat cat, me being one of them. I knew things would be different once I walked in on Vanessa changing into her gym clothes.

Damn I hated going to gym, always the same ass boring shit, run laps, climb the rope, do this and do that. I walked in the locker room and Vanessa was already in there. We speak all the time, we just never really hung out. And when I say she was a sexy looking young woman, I mean she had my attention. Her skin was milk chocolate smooth, she always wore her hair in a pony tail that swung right at the nape of her neck. Her body was toned mainly because she was on the track team. Her breast were full, she didn't have a real curvy ass which I was fine with either way.

When I entered the locker room she didn't have on a shirt. I was able to take notice of her full size breast; she was just changing into her gym clothes.

"Oh hey what's going on Sunni." I went to my locker to start undressing.

"It's all good over here. Rather be anywhere else than in this gym class."

"I hear that. I hate gym. You have to run around in a fucking circle just to get an A. What kind of shit is that?"

"Indeed. That's why I don't think I'm coming tomorrow, I don't have time for this boring shit. It's not like I'm going to fail anyway, my passing grade is on lock."

"And how did you pull that shit off? Because if I don't come, I don't pass."

"It's simple. It's all about who you know and who you do." I slammed my locker door closed and walked into the gym area.

Giving the fact that she and I made intense eye contact all the while we were talking let me know she was down to get her lick-her-license.

Five days later I was stretched eagle on my sofa

and she finally got her license, damn she really

earned that mother fucker too.

Cleaning house

When I walked into the house Sunni was already laying in the sofa and that's right where I left her ass. I didn't want to wake her and hear all that whinny ass baby talk she does whenever she's addressing me. I made it safely to our bedroom. I took my clothes off and just laid in the bed. I'm so ready to be done with all of the bullshit. I texted Lou a month ago and she still hasn't responded which I figured she wouldn't. All that means is that it's time for me to contact her again and this time it won't be texting. This time I'm calling so I can make sure I hear her voice, granted if she don't hang up in my face.

Laying in my King size bed alone looking up at the ceiling, the street light is letting just a little light in. One arm under my head, the other across my stomach. Thinking about Lou got me ready to call her now. I know it's late and I know the best thing is to wait until morning. I surely don't want to deal with Sunni ass so I think I'll call on my way to work.

Lou was suppose too be the only female in this house; no one else. I can honestly say I fucked that up and there really was no need, I could just have lived solo and fucked Sunni whenever the opportunity presented its self which seems to be a lot when Sunni is involved.

I glanced at the red numbers on the night stand clock seeing that it is 2:30 in the morning. I tried to stay out later. Now that I'm home, I should've stayed out later but I'll be damned if I let Sunni keep me from my own house. It's just a matter of time. Wait, scratch that. It's only a matter of days that I send little Miss Sunshine back to her own home for good. Shit if I had any sense I would have dipped across the street to my friendly neighbor house and let her put me to sleep. I won't lie, her sex is good. Not great but damn it, I'll hit it again. My hand is itching to call up Lou but if she hang up on me I'm subject to go over to her house tonight.

Fuck it! I'm a man about my shit and I think the quickest way to let Sunni know that the time has come for her to bounce is to simply call Lou. I grabbed my phone quick off the nightstand, went to my contacts and clicked on her number. I started feeling a little nervous when I heard the phone ring.

"Hello." Her voice was low, barely above a whisper.

"Hello my lady Lou."

"Devin?"

"Yes." That's when I expected to hear the phone click.

"You do know that it is dark thirty?"

"Yes but I really need to talk to you and I didn't want to wait any longer. Too much time has passed and I should have corrected this wrong a long time ago." The silence that my ears heard was about to drive me insane in just a short amount of time.

"Well as usual I don't mind you calling. And yes it has been too damn long on both of our parts. How about tomorrow you come to the shop? I open up at ten but I'll get there at nine so we can talk." When I heard those words escape her lips I couldn't have been happier if I was a child waking up on Christmas morning.

"I'll see you at nine Lou and thanks for answering the phone." I heard her do a faint laugh before she hung up.

She didn't have to say a damn word. Just her answering was enough for me, lets me know that I can go get my woman back.

******

I know this mother fucker isn't in here on the phone talking to Lou. I know my ears are not hearing this shit. I heard him when he came in and walked right pass me. I didn't really care. I've been knowing what it is between both of us for a while now. We both knew that moving in together was a no-no but because we had our own reasons of doing so, went through with it. Moving in with Devin didn't give the results I had hoped it would. I wanted his precious Lou to go into a deep depression, lose her fucking mind. I see she was stronger than I thought. I know for a fact that over this pass year they haven't been in contact until recently, maybe as only recent as tonight.

I knew this day would come, I just didn't know how soon. I'm willing to walk away because I'm not gaining nothing from being with Devin. I have my own house, car, and most importantly money; a shit load of it. Devin is a cool guy but all this falling in love and wanting to be married shit at a young age is bullshit. He got a big dick. He better go out there and swing it before he actually does settle down.

Devin really thought I cared about people knowing my secret of fucking the whole football team and basketball team back in Texas. Now that I'm grown, I really don't give a fuck who knows. Hell, even his home boy Terry knows, and many more; point blank. If you have come to any one of my orgy parties it was no secret that my illness is the reason why we having this party. It's a good thing too because I don't have to hide and sneak my shit. It is what it is and everyone who comes anywhere near my home is practically like me. And I'm okay with that. I have always known in my life that no man will ever wife me because of my sexual activity and that's okay. I'm not trying to be tied down by marriage, it's a whole fucking world out here. Maybe when I am older, much older, I'll move somewhere where no one knows me and start over. But for now I am having fun going through Chicago.

I fucked around and got pregnant, no worries though. I'm not keeping it and Terry don't want it either. The only reason I know its Terry's because he's the only person I don't use protection with. Devin ass started using protection damn near as soon as I moved in which further lets me know that he had an issue with me being so damn sexual. Like I've always said that's his problem not mine.

I was prepared to go back home before I heard Devin talking to Lou. Now that I know for sure he's going back in that direction I'm really ready to go back home to my home. When I heard Devin talking to Lou I wanted to scream down on him. Then I thought at this point, it don't even make sense to do so. He knows and have known for a while that I've been doing me, it's not like I hide everything from him. Random fucks, yes I don't speak on but people like Terry and anyone else I think he may know, yes I do tell him about them. I never want him to feel like he has just walked into an ambush.

I did have fun with Devin, this gives me a sense of what a real relationship feels like. I know he wants one so bad, some people are just into the whole relationship monogamous thing; I'm not one of them.

I wish Devin all the best in the world as for me this is where I exit stage left.

Back on track

I couldn't believe my eyes when Devin walked into the shop a couple of weeks ago. I think I smiled so damn hard I got my ears wet. There was a little bit of awkwardness in the room but as mad as I wanted to be at him, I just couldn't. Time has passed that we can't get back.

I could have said and did so many rotten things to him just to piss him off then our relationship wouldn't be as strong as it is now. I didn't know what to really expect when he came to the shop, I just knew I was going to listen. We talked even after the shop was open. It was a slow day so I wasn't bombarded with customers. We were able to sit and find a happy medium.

I have let everyone go or at the very least downsized them to just a friend. I want to show Devin that it's not that I don't and never wanted a relationship with him. I just wasn't ready to finish swimming in the pond of men. But this last year without him has let me know that my fear of being cheated on has nothing to do with him but everything to do with me.

I want to be with him and I've let him know this very thing we have practically growing up together, I want us to continue to grow. The last few weeks Devin has let me know that little Miss Sunshine has moved out and took her ass back to her own home. Devin has tried to let me know the reasons behind what he did and honestly I had to stop him. I'm not a dummy, I knew why. I just think it was definitely done in poor taste. Like momma says a man has to get his own shit straight before he can make it right with you.

I love Devin, always have. And this is where he has me stepping my game up. To make this work I must say, my game is on point.

****

Damn, I can't believe that I've been away from this woman for a whole damn year. When I walked in the shop I could have hit the floor, her beauty slapped the shit out of me. This woman has always had my heart and she knows it. I wanted to tell her right then and there how sorry I was and try and explain my reason for doing what I was doing. Lou didn't want to hear any of it, she says she understands even though she didn't like it, she didn't want to rehash any of last year's events.

Lou and I have spoken about any and everything that has led up to this moment. Her actions shows me that she really wants to give us a real try. I never thought we would see this day so soon, but I do know that absence does makes the heart grow founder.

I have asked her to move in but she said not without redecorating. I knew what she meant. No woman wants to smell the remnants of another woman lingering around.

As for Ms. Sunni, I hear she's doing what she loves which is doing her, with no one to answer to. Hey, I must say if she ever get that monkey off her back she'll be a good wife but until then she'll be making sure many men and women have a good nut. That's all she has to offer, sad too.

Like most men, if they're true friends they talk about any and everything. When Terry told me about the baby and that she in fact did have an abortion I didn't care either way. I was just glad it wasn't mine.

I have loved Lou for a long time and I guess when you actually know then you know.

I didn't need a whole lot of women to satisfy me; I only needed one.